He was having the unfortunate and powerful effect of making Bridget completely addled.

Which she'd been from the moment she'd opened her door, looked *way* up and seen him push his fingers through the chocolate silk of his hair. His eyes had been mesmerizing—a mix of gold and green, with a light burning in them that even she could see was frank male appreciation.

The light had said Justin didn't see her as little Miss Librarian, despite the severity of her hairdo and the straight lines of her skirt. Somehow he had seen through all that as if it was nothing more than a disguise—a role she played. He had seen her as a woman and something shockingly primal in her had answered back.

Which was dreadful, of course. Because it went without saying that he was the kind of man she absolutely loathed.

D0288402

Dear Reader,

Whether you're enjoying one of the first snowfalls of the season or lounging in a beach chair at some plush island resort, I hope you've got some great books by your side. I'm especially excited about the Silhouette Romance titles this month as we're kicking off 2006 with two great new miniseries by some of your all-time favorite authors.

Cara Colter teams up with her daughter, Cassidy Caron, to launch our new PERPETUALLY YOURS trilogy. *In Love's Nine Lives* (#1798) a beautiful librarian's extremely possessive tabby tries to thwart a budding romance between *his* mistress and a man who seems all wrong for her but is anything but. Teresa Southwick returns with *That Touch of Pink* (#1799)—the first in her BUY-A-GUY trilogy. When a single mom literally buys a former military man at a bachelor auction to help her daughter earn a wilderness badge, she gets a lot more than she bargained for...and is soon earning points toward *her own* romantic survival badge. Old sparks turn into an all-out blaze when the hero returns to the family ranch in *Sometimes When We Kiss* (#1800) by Linda Goodnight. Finally, Elise Mayr debuts with *The Rancher's Redemption* (#1801) in which a widow, desperate to help her sick daughter, throws herself on the mercy of her commanding brother-in-law whose eyes reflect anything but the hate she'd expected.

And be sure to come back next month for more great reading, with Sandra Paul's distinctive addition to the PERPETUALLY YOURS trilogy and Judy Christenberry's new madcap mystery.

Have a very happy and healthy 2006.

Ann Leslie Tuttle
Associate Senior Editor

Please address questions and book requests to:
Silhouette Reader Service
U.S.: 3010 Walden Ave., P.O. Box 1325, Buffalo, NY 14269
Canadian: P.O. Box 609, Fort Erie, Ont. L2A 5X3

CARA COLTER
CASSIDY CARON

LOVE'S
NINE LIVES

PerPetually
Yours

SILHOUETTE *Romance*®

Published by Silhouette Books

America's Publisher of Contemporary Romance

This one is for Hunter.
Without you, this book, and so much more,
would not be possible.
Thank you for all the lessons and laughter.
Who knew so much joy could come from one small being?

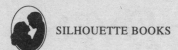 **SILHOUETTE BOOKS**

ISBN 0-373-19798-5

LOVE'S NINE LIVES

Copyright © 2006 by Collette Caron and Cassidy Caron

This edition published by arrangement with Harlequin Books S.A.

® and TM are trademarks of Harlequin Books S.A., used under license.
Trademarks indicated with ® are registered in the United States Patent
and Trademark Office, the Canadian Trade Marks Office and in other
countries.

Visit Silhouette Books at www.eHarlequin.com

Printed in U.S.A.

Books by Cara Colter

Silhouette Romance

Dare To Dream #491
Baby in Blue #1161
Husband in Red #1243
The Cowboy, the Baby
  and the Bride-To-Be #1319
Truly Daddy #1363
A Bride Worth Waiting For #1388
Weddings Do Come True #1406
A Babe in the Woods #1424
A Royal Marriage #1440
First Time, Forever #1464
**Husband by Inheritance* #1532
**The Heiress Takes a Husband* #1538

*Wed by a Will #1544
What Child Is This? #1585
Her Royal Husband #1600
9 Out of 10 Women Can't Be
  Wrong #1615
Guess Who's Coming for
  Christmas? #1632
What a Woman Should
  Know #1685
Major Daddy #1710
Her Second-Chance Man #1726
Nighttime Sweethearts #1754
Love's Nine Lives #1798

*The Wedding Legacy

Silhouette Books

The Coltons
A Hasty Wedding

CARA COLTER

shares her life with the man of her dreams, her spirited teenage daughter, Cassidy Caron, several spotted horses and a fiery orange tabby cat. Her perfect day includes writing, riding and reading. Cara has weaknesses for Tim Horton's iced cappuccino (a true Canadian pleasure), English toffee coffee and high-quality chocolate (the only known remedy for writer's block). Working with her daughter to create this story was one of the most gratifying experiences of her career.

CASSIDY CARON

Eighteen-year-old high school student Cass Caron has been an extraordinary explorer of the Canadian wilderness. She has participated in grueling back-country treks, horse-pack trips and fly-in adventures. Cass has sold articles to outdoor publications, trained horses and worked in an orchard. She loves cats and is frequently inspired by them. Her dreams for her future include a high action outdoor career and a man who cooks!

CONAN'S "TO DO" LIST

1. CAT NAP.

2. INSPECT LITTER BOX.

3. CAT NAP.

4. EXERCISE — HALF LAP AROUND KITCHEN TABLE.

5. SNACK — BOYCOTT DIET CAT FOOD. BUTTER SHOULD BE ON COUNTER.

6. **# 1 URGENT:** FOIL ANY ATTEMPT BY JUSTIN "THE PEST" WEST TO ROMANCE MISS BRIDGET DAISY.

Chapter One

"Conan, please."

He curled his tail more tightly around his body and squinched his eyes shut, feigning sleep. Unless she was offering sautéed shrimp, she could forget it.

"Conan, just try one little bite."

Something disgusting was wafted in front of his nose.

Diet cat treats. Ha, as if the words *diet* and *treat* could be used successfully together. He opened one eye, glared at his mistress and then snapped it shut again.

"Conan, you know what the vet said. You are a tiny bit overweight."

The vet was a horrible old man who smelled overwhelmingly of dogs. As if that wasn't bad enough, the good doctor's body odor and breath gave away an even more treacherous secret: vegetarian.

The veterinarian was a dog-loving vegetarian, and she was going to take diet advice from him? The man knew nothing about the delicacies of dealing with a cat, that had been obvious.

He heard his mistress walk away, so Conan opened one eye, placing an orange-colored paw carefully over it so he could watch her unobserved.

He felt momentarily contrite. Her copper-colored hair, usually so neatly put back into a bun, was hanging loose around her face. Her green eyes were wide with worry, and there was a wrinkle in her normally unblemished forehead. She was still in her pajamas, something unheard of, even if it was Sunday morning.

She was obviously distressed, and it made Conan realize that she really was not as confident or mature as her primly done hair and straight-lined business suits suggested. Really he was partly to blame for that visit to the vet.

Okay, fully to blame. He'd been a free-roaming tabby his entire sorry life, until he'd found himself in lockup and had been rescued by her late last fall.

At first he thought he must have used up his ninth life, even though he'd been counting pretty carefully and thought he was only on seven. For it had seemed, after being adopted from the Hunter's Corner Pet Shelter, that he must have died and gone to heaven!

Miss Bridget Daisy was one of the few people he'd ever met who really deserved to own a cat. First the name: Conan. Celtic for "mighty one," she'd explained to him after days of making lists and debating over just the right name. Really, what could have been more suiting? The mighty one. Perfect.

And then the food! She was constantly delighting him: roasted chicken livers, succulent steak bits and his all-time favorite, sautéed shrimp.

Okay, okay, things were not perfect, even in heaven. When winter had come she had presented him with a sweater with his name on it. And a horrid little hat. A guy should have had way more pride, but he had a weakness for the shrimp. Miss Daisy might look innocent, but she knew how to play a guy's weaknesses.

Right now, having been shrimp-deprived for three whole days, he'd probably wear a tutu for one small morsel of seafood, any variety.

But the biggest problem with coming home to Miss Daisy hadn't been the clothes, as humiliating as they were. No, it had been the fact that she wouldn't let him outside without a leash. A leash! Of course, in the winter, who wanted to go outside anyway? Winters were made for snoozing on the couch. But spring changed everything…

Which brought him to the visit with Dr. Veggie, the vet.

Conan had been perched in one of his favorite places—on the back of her couch—minding his own business, really.

And then the bird had landed at the feeder, a location that had seen dismally little traffic over the winter but was looking more promising now. The front-yard feeder was shaped like a little house, with shutters and cute signs all over it that said things like Open for Business and Birds Welcome. As if birds could read! The expression *birdbrained* had not manifested out of thin air.

The bird at the feeder had been a purple finch, something Conan adored even more than shrimp, if that was possible. He felt finch had the most delectable flavor—slightly wild and faintly smoky with just a touch of bitter aftertaste, probably from the feathers.

In no time at all, focused with hunter intensity on the bird, Conan had totally forgotten the window. He had gone into a crouch, his tail switching, his eyes narrowed on the prey. He'd waited, knowing the bird would make a mistake, land on the ground, greedy thing, wanting that one more tiny seed....

There it was. His moment. Even as he'd launched himself, he'd heard her voice in the background.

"Conaaaan, nooooo!"

Too late.

He'd bounced back off that window as if he was a tennis ball spiked from a racket and lay on the floor dazed, blood—important blood, his—splattering the carpet around him.

Hence the unfortunate meeting with Dr. Veggie, a white-haired antiquity with more wrinkles and creases than that Shar-Pei monstrosity Conan had been forced to share the waiting room with. Conan had hated the little winter balaclava Miss Daisy had made for him, but he hated this more—his whole head wound with white tape, his ears poking through two holes in the top, his face completely surrounded in white as if he were a nun wearing a wimple.

It was horrible. And was there a little sautéed shrimp to help him through his most humiliating moment? No, there was not.

Because the evil dog lover had pronounced him

overweight. Nothing so scientific as a scale either. Just prodding with those poochie-smelling fingers that had been God knew where else that morning!

Miss Daisy could be counted on to be thorough, though. She had taken him home and put him on her bathroom scale. He should have known her gasp of dismay did not bode well for his culinary endeavors. She had actually thought the scale wasn't working.

"Twenty-six pounds! Conan, I don't think that's possible."

Of course it wasn't possible. He was a little portly, not fat. It was not at all his fault. His mother had also been big-boned.

But then Miss Daisy had weighed herself, and it seemed the scale had been correct after all.

So now he lay curled on the couch, looking like a cat extra for *The Mummy* and feeling slightly crazed from food deprivation. It was a low point in his life, he decided. He'd had a sniff of the diet food she'd put out and decided it was worth sulking for a few more days to see if he could make her come around.

He heard her pick up the phone and perked up slightly.

Maybe she was giving in. Would the pizza joint be open at eleven o'clock on Sunday morning? He got the pepperoni nicely gobbed with melted cheese, and she got the inedible portions—tomato paste and crust. There was simply no figuring humans.

"Dr. Thornfield?"

Conan groaned and put his head back down.

"It's Bridget Daisy. I'm sorry to bother you at home. I'm calling about Conan." There was a long pause. "No, no, his head seems fine. No, no blood seeping through the bandages. Of course it doesn't stink!"

The man was gross. Couldn't he word things more delicately than that?

Her voice went very low, as if she didn't want Conan to hear, but he was a cat, which meant superior hearing. Superior everything, come to that.

"I think he's depressed," she whispered into the phone.

Yes! Depressed. Treat immediately with vanilla ice cream, with just a little shrimpy-poo on top.

Miss Daisy was quiet for a moment and then when she spoke, her voice had an unfamiliar icy note in it.

"I can't believe you said that! You think I need to occupy myself? A husband? A child?"

Conan winced and barely staved off a painful flashback from his former life. Oh, no, he did not care for husbands or for children, and look how quickly she had taken the dieting advice!

But he needn't have worried. Her voice was now quite loud, shrill even.

"What a totally unprofessional thing to say! I thought you were a man of education and refinement. I can see now I was wrong. You are—"

Conan held his breath, waiting, delighted. *You give it to him, Miss Daisy,* he thought. He was streetwise enough to have various phrases at hand that he would have loved to hear her use on the evil dog-loving, diet-prescribing Dr. Veggie.

"You are—" her voice quivered with righteous anger "—hopelessly old-fashioned!"

Disappointment washed over Conan. Sheesh. Hopelessly old-fashioned? What about *You are a dog-breathed poop eater?* What about *You are a birdbrained worm slurper?* Sometimes Conan wondered if there was any hope at all for Miss Daisy.

She marched into the living room. "Why," she said, her voice still quivering with indignation, "he's just another barbarian. Just like all the rest of them in this town."

Ah, yes, Conan had heard quite a lot about the town's barbarians. That was how Miss Daisy referred to the male population. Beer-swilling barbarians whose idea of culture was growing in the bottom of their lunch pails. According to Miss Daisy, every single man in Hunter's Corner, Ohio, loved duck hunting and fishing and playing pool. The name of the place should have given her a clue. Redneck heaven.

Duck hunting usually involved dogs of some sort, so Conan was against that, but he thought she might have been too quick to write off fishing. A nice freshly caught trout, braised in butter and garlic, was nothing to turn up one's nose at!

He had no opinion on pool, but if it was one of the reasons Miss Daisy had ended up at the animal shelter seeking companionship, he could hardly condemn it.

She never really said she was lonely, but Conan could tell. She'd told him most of her life story his first night in residence, curled up together on the sofa, her popping little soft-centered nondiet cat treats into his mouth as she talked.

She was from Boston and had a master's degree in library science. When she'd been offered the position of librarian here, in this northeastern corner of Ohio, right after completing university, she had jumped at the opportunity.

"Of course," she had told Conan that night, "I always thought I'd move on. To a bigger place, a city bursting with art and live theater and music. To a place with corner cafés that serve lattes, quaint little bookstores filled with old treasures and outdoor flower markets."

She sighed heavily and pulled him more tightly into her bosom. "But, Conan, I have come to love my little brick library across from the town square. I've done so much with it in the two years I've been here! We have story time and a poetry club. The chess club meets there once a week. Why, the collection is marvelous for a small-town library! How could I leave it?"

Still, he could see her dilemma. How was a woman like her ever going to find companionship in a town where men drove pickup trucks with wheels nearly the size of her house?

At the animal shelter, of course!

Barring the sweater, hat and leash, it had not been an unhappy arrangement, really, until the last three days. Now Conan wasn't so sure if it was going to work.

"I've got it," she said suddenly, squatting down by the couch and running her hands tenderly through his fur. "I know how to make you happy."

He sighed with relief. Their first fight over, then. Of course she knew how to make him happy.

She was reaching for the phone book. Oh, goody. That meant takeout. Perhaps she had just realized the calamari was calorie-reduced. With a nice little side of salt-and-pepper squid… He began to purr happily.

She was frowning at the phone book. "How do I find a contractor?" she muttered. "Every single one of them will take one look at me and realize I'm a woman alone. I'll be overcharged for shoddy workmanship."

What the heck was she talking about? What did any of that have to do with honey-glazed salmon?

"I'll ask Fred, the maintenance man at the library," she decided, closing the telephone book.

Conan willed her to reopen it to the Yellow Pages, Restaurants, but she did not.

Instead she picked him up as if he didn't weigh anything near twenty-six pounds and waltzed around the room with him tucked next to her heart.

"Conan," she announced, "you are getting a cat door!"

His disappointment was sharp. A cat door was a long, long way from the little tuna sushi rolls that he favored.

"I'll have it installed in the back door and I'll have the fence replaced around the yard and then you can go outside and play while I'm at work. I won't have to worry about you going over the fence either."

My God, she thought he was too chubby to drag himself over a fence?

He glared at her, but she was oblivious to his mood, dancing around, blabbering about drawing up specifications.

Her mood was hard to resist, however, and suddenly it struck him what he was being offered.

Freedom. The great outdoors in springtime.

She had bird feeders everywhere in that backyard! It would be like having his very own drive-through window.

I'll have the McFinch, please.

Conan chuckled to himself. It came out as a deep, rich purr, and his mistress hugged him tighter.

"I knew I could make you happy," she said blissfully.

Justin West hopped out of his truck and eyed the house. It was in the older part of Hunter's Corner, a neighborhood called Honeysuckle, where small, post-age-stamp-size houses sat on huge lots surrounded by the neighborhood's namesake. At this time of year the air smelled sweet with the scent of the blossoms that hung heavy in the shrubbery.

This house was extremely well kept, the shingle sid-ing painted sunshine-yellow, the trim, stairs and win-dow boxes white. Cheerful red geraniums were already planted in those boxes. A front window was open and a lace curtain danced on the light spring breeze.

"Thanks, Fred," Justin muttered.

Justin owned West's Construction, a construction company specializing in framing new houses. The north side of town was building up phenomenally as more and more people left the cities looking for exactly what Hunter's Corner, population fifteen thousand, had to offer—a small-town feel and flavor.

There was no Wal-Mart, no Starbucks, no multiplex theaters. The town was tidy, safe and neighborly. For amenities, it boasted a town square with a park that chil-dren still played in. There was a library, a swimming pool that was open in the summer, two grocery stores, one ice cream parlor and close proximity to the great outdoors and all its attractions. People here sat on their front porches, grew gardens, threw out a fishing pole in their spare time. Kids rode their bikes down the tree-lined streets and walked unescorted to school.

Justin West had more work than he knew what to do with.

He didn't need the kind of job a tidy house in Honeysuckle implied—a little old lady who wanted a new washstand for the backyard. He'd be plied with cookies and tea—and get phone calls long after the job was done about imaginary popped nails or squeaks. When he arrived to investigate, there would be more cookies and tea and pictures of the new grandchild.

On the other hand, Fred had asked him to come and at least look at the job. And how could he say no to Fred?

In his seventies, Fred was still the town maintenance man, refusing to reveal his actual age or to consider retirement. He had also been Justin's father's best friend since the days when Hunter's Corner had been little more than an autumn retreat for city boys who wanted to bag a deer or two. Fred had been there through all those lonely, hard years when the Alzheimer's took hold, wrapped its tentacles around Justin's father's mind, changing him from a powerful man into a baffled, helpless child. Fred had never once said, "I'm too busy," when Justin called in panic because he had to be at work and his dad was having one of "those" days.

His dad had gone finally, a bittersweet blessing. And now Fred was asking a favor of him, of Justin, for a lady friend.

Justin wasn't going to return the friendship and loyalty that Fred had shown his father with *I'm too busy,* even though he was.

Justin took the front steps two at a time, knocked on the door—loudly, in case Fred's lady friend was deaf. He thought it was nice that Fred had a lady friend. Fred's wife had been gone for nearly fifteen years. And his best friend for just over a year. It was about time—

The door opened, and Justin reeled back, nearly stumbling off the step. He grabbed the handrail and steadied himself.

The woman smiling tentatively at him was shockingly beautiful, maybe particularly in contrast to his expectation that the door was going to be opened by someone old and wrinkled and deaf.

Justin gauged her to be in her mid to late twenties. She had hair the exact color of shiny new copper, pulled back quite severely off her face. But the severity of the hairstyle only emphasized the loveliness of her features: high cheekbones, a pert nose, a small tilted chin, a gloriously generous mouth. There was the slightest smattering of freckles over milky-white skin, and eyes that were huge and green as Smoky's Pond on a summer afternoon. She was slender as a reed and petite, the kind of woman that gave a man the dangerous feeling that he was big and strong and that he had been put on this earth for the sole purpose of protecting those more fragile than himself.

She had an enormous orange cat in her arms that was comically bandaged around its head. Justin had a feeling it might be a mistake to laugh at the cat, which was glaring at him with baleful dislike. She juggled its bulk to offer a slender hand.

"Justin West?" she asked.

He took a steadying breath and accepted her hand. It

was cool and soft and small—and packed a jolt like a shock from a circular saw with a bad connection in a rainstorm. He held her grip a fraction longer than might have been necessary. The cat shifted its weight, forcing her to withdraw her hand or let the cat slide down her front.

"I'm Bridget Daisy. Thank you for coming."

So he did have the right address. She was Fred's friend, though obviously not his lady friend in the way Justin had imagined. He glanced at her ring finger. Bare. Lord have mercy!

"Come in."

He stepped by her, aware of a lovely fragrance, light and sweet, as he moved directly into her living room. The room increased his sense of being big and male, clumsy and uncouth. There were trinkets, potted plants, a vase of fresh flowers on the floor at the edge of the couch. If he breathed, he was going to break something.

"Have a seat," she suggested.

Where? Everything in the room was small and frail-looking, not man-size at all. The tiny sofa was set on curvy legs and was covered in a fabric that looked suspiciously like ivory silk that would be destroyed by his just-finished-work-for-the-day jeans and T-shirt.

His gaze caught on an old leather wingback that looked slightly sturdier than her other furniture. The chair was rump sprung, as if it was the favored spot of someone with a little more meat on their bones than her. Justin beelined for it, but her delicate cough stopped him just short of sitting down. He glanced back at her.

She smiled apologetically. "That's Conan's chair."

Conan? He felt a wave of relieved disappointment. Ring fingers didn't really tell the story these days. But he should have known a girl like her came with a guy named Conan. Muscle-bound. Big. Territorial. Couldn't the roommate build her washstand or whatever she wanted?

She moved by him and set the cat in the chair. "Isn't that right, Conan?"

Conan was the cat? The cat inspected the spot carefully, turned two full circles, then plopped himself down. The chair groaned, and the cat gave Justin a look of naked dislike, as if it was somehow his fault the chair was making noises. Then Conan dismissed their visitor by delicately lifting his tail and beginning his bath.

"I didn't want you to get hair on your clothes," Miss Bridget Daisy told him.

He looked down at his clothes. Like a little cat hair would hurt? But she gestured to the sofa, and he reluctantly perched on the corner, trying to make as little contact with the highly soilable silk as possible.

She took the far end of the same sofa, and now that she wasn't hiding behind the cat, he could see she was wearing a businesslike suit in an unflattering color that flattered her nonetheless. Despite her slenderness, she had curves in all the right places. When she sat down, the tight skirt edged up, revealing the most adorable little kneecap.

"Sorry?" he said, realizing she was saying something.

"Thank you for coming on such short notice. Fred said you were very busy. How do you know him?"

"He's my godfather. He and my dad were best friends since they were kids."

She folded her hands primly over that delicate little knee and regarded him solemnly. "How long have you been building, Mr. West?"

"Justin," he corrected her. "Uh, ever since I can remember. It's a family business. Between my grandad, my dad and me, we've built just about every building in town."

"Oh." She looked very pleased by that. She slid a little clipboard out from behind one of the cushions and made a mark on it. "So is your work guaranteed, then?"

He realized, stunned, that he had somehow become an involuntary participant in a job interview. He ordered himself to wake up and quit looking at her kneecap, to take charge of this situation by letting her know in no uncertain terms he wasn't going to be insulted with an interview. That's not how it worked.

He came in, looked at the job, gave her a price. Take it or leave it. Unfortunately her eyes were every bit as distracting as her kneecap.

"I stand behind my work," he said shortly.

"Of course you'd sign something saying that?"

Devastating kneecaps and eyes aside, he could feel himself starting to get annoyed. "What kind of job do you have?" he asked. He hadn't even said he'd do the job, and she was talking about signing something? He had houses to build. He was doing her a favor by being here!

Almost shyly she reached behind her pillow again and came out with a thick manila folder, which she passed to him. The shyness—her dropping her thick lashes over the amazing green of her eyes rather than holding his gaze—made him bite back his annoyance and take the folder.

"This is my project prospectus," she told him happily, meeting his eyes briefly before looking away. Was she blushing?

He tore his eyes away from the heightened color in her cheeks and felt the weight of what had been passed into his hands. It was thicker than the Hunter's Corner telephone directory. What the hell was her project? A new shopping mall? The Taj Mahal comes to Ohio?

He opened the cover of the folder. A full-color eight-by-ten glossy of the cat was clipped to the first page. In the photo the cat was wearing a knitted purple sweater and he looked none too happy about it either.

Justin shot Bridget Daisy a wary look. Was she nuts? What a shame that would be, but of course that would explain why a woman this gorgeous but single had gone undetected on the Hunter's Corner bachelor radar. Not that, God forbid, he was on the lookout for single women. After having had responsibility for his ailing father since high school, Justin West was enjoying freedom.

Getting tied down would not be his idea of a good time.

An evening with those kneecaps, though, no strings attached…

He looked hurriedly down at her "prospectus."

"I'll go make us tea while you have a look at that."

"Great," he muttered, but kissed his fantasy of an evening with her kneecaps goodbye. Tea? If the offer had been for a beer or, better yet, a whiskey, there might have been hope, but he could see there was not. She was not his kind of woman.

While she busied herself in the kitchen, he reviewed a two-page letter that invited him to study the Statement of Work—in brackets, SOW—for the installation of a Cat Door and Yard Fence and then sign the Contract for Work (COW) if he was in agreement with the SOW.

With growing consternation he studied her invitation. Lettered from A to I, she required a firm price, payment schedules, commencement dates and completion dates, warranties of workmanship and materials, proof of insurance, four references and any other information he felt might be pertinent.

He listened to the kettle whistle in the kitchen, eyed the door, thought of Fred and took a deep breath. He opened page one of her twelve-page Statement of Work.

On page three he got it suddenly. He peeked up from the document and saw her in her kitchen arranging cookies on a plate.

He slid a look around the living room. There had to be a hidden camera somewhere. The guys loved a practical joke, and this was a good one. Imagine them roping Fred into playing a part in getting him here. Pure genius, that one. This probably wasn't even her house. She was an actress, maybe even a professional one, though Justin wasn't sure how you went about finding someone like that in Hunter's Corner. He decided he'd play along until she said, "Smile, you're on...".

She came back in with a silver tea tray and set it on the coffee table. The teacups looked as though they held about a thimbleful of tea, which suited Justin just fine. He wasn't much of a tea drinker. He watched, reluctantly fascinated, as she poured. He didn't think the queen could do it any better.

"Have you had a chance to look things over?" she asked eagerly, passing him a cup and a saucer. When he took it, the tea sloshed out of the cup. The cup was flimsy, as if it was looking for an excuse to shatter, and his fingers did not fit through the wispy little handles the way hers did. He could only hope it was a prop.

"This is a complicated job," he said solemnly. He took a sip of tea and tried not to wince at the bitter, weedy flavor, since he was sure that would entertain the guys more when they reviewed their videotape. He set the cup down, locked his hands together and leaned intently toward Bridget.

"You probably didn't know that the construction of the door affects the integrity of the structure of the house. It won't be cheap."

"That's what I thought," she said sadly.

God, she was good. The guys must have the tape running. He hoped so. Because he planned to have the last laugh when they all looked at it together later.

"For instance, this—" he flipped randomly to page four of the SOW "—about R28 insulation? That would make the depth of the cat door at least eight inches. And heavy. Not even Mr. Hefty over there could push it open."

"Mr. Hefty?" she said. Her voice had a little squeak in it that seemed quite genuine and her eyes sparked with indignation that looked real.

"Not to worry," he assured her. "All problems are surmountable. We'd have to install an electronic opener."

"For a cat door?"

"Well, you're the one who specified R28," he pointed out not unkindly, playing to the camera that he just knew was in here somewhere.

"I didn't realize that would make the door quite so cumbersome," she admitted.

She talked like a girl with a college education. Yeah, majoring in drama. She was frowning and looking anxious.

Playing it perfectly. And the Academy Award goes to…

He ignored the distressed look and flipped to another page of the SOW. "And this part here, about preventing rodent infestation? You have to take it further than that. You have to think of skunks and raccoons. Even a small break-and-enter artist—one of those young kids who hang around the park at night—might be able to squeeze through."

"I hadn't thought of that," she said nervously.

"No, ma'am. I can see that. Twelve pages of SOW and you missed the obvious. Luckily I have a solution."

"You do?" she said hopefully.

"Yes, ma'am. I think we could rig a computer system that identifies your cat, and your cat only, by his nose print."

She went very still. Comprehension dawned in her eyes. After a long time she said very softly, "Are you making fun of me, Mr. West?"

"Hell, yeah!" She winced when he said *hell.* "The game's up. I know the guys put you up to this. A twelve-page prospectus for a cat door! Ha-ha."

He slapped his knee, but noticed uncomfortably that Miss Bridget Daisy was not laughing.

Chapter Two

Bridget stared at the big man, and she was struck again by how his big, powerful hand was making her tea-cup—a lovely Royal Doulton that she had inherited from her grandmother—look like a toy.

He was having the same effect on her sofa. With his huge frame jammed into the corner of it, a sofa she had always been perfectly content with suddenly seemed as though it belonged in a dollhouse.

In fact, Justin West, in the short time he had been there, was having the unfortunate and powerful effect of making it seem as if her whole life was make-believe, as if she had been playing with toys and imaginary friends and here was the real thing.

Justin West was real, all right. The man was one hundred per cent real—huge, handsome and infuriatingly male. She had felt addled from the moment she had opened the door, looked *way* up and seen him push his fingers through the chocolate silk of his hair. His eyes had been absolutely mesmerizing—a mix of gold and green, with a light burning in them that even she could see was frank male appreciation.

That light said Justin didn't see her as little Miss Librarian, despite the severity of her hairdo and the straight lines of her skirt. Somehow he had seen through all that as if it was nothing more than a disguise—a role she played. He had seen her as a woman, and something shockingly primal in her had answered back.

Oh, not in words, thank God. In awareness. She had felt as though she sat on her edge of the couch practically quivering with nervous awareness—the easy play of his muscles; his scent, wild and intoxicating as high mountain meadows; the light in his eyes; the husky, deep sensuality of his voice.

Which was dreadful, of course. Because it went without saying that Justin West was the kind of man she absolutely loathed: full of himself, sure of his own attractions, shallow as a mud puddle. He would be just like all those athletic boys in high school and college who had known she was alive only long enough to poke fun at her. Justin West was one of the happy heathens of Hunter's Corner.

Any small and secret hope that he might be different somehow than the other redneck men of this town were dashed. If Justin was really *different* she would have seen him at the library where the more refined citizens tended to gather. And she had never seen *this* man in *her* library.

This man thought the cat door was some sort of joke. He was making fun of her, just the way all those handsome, cocky boys in high school and beyond had always made fun of her.

Miss Priss. Four-Eyes. Brainiac.

As if there was something shameful about being smart. The painful taunts came back as though he had uttered them...and so did her feeling of helpless fury, not that she would ever allow him to see it. In her experience, showing vulnerability only made things worse.

With as much dignity as she could muster she said, "I don't know what guys you are talking about, Mr. West."

"Probably Harry Burnside, right?"

"Harry Burnside?" she said coolly. "I'm afraid I don't know anyone by that name."

"Yeah, right." But doubt flickered across his features, and he looked down at her carefully prepared folder and frowned. "Well, come to think of it, I'm not sure Harry could spell *infestation*. Or *rodent*."

"And this is a friend of yours?" she asked, her tone deliberately controlled, faintly *judgmental*. Given the unsteady hammering of her heart, she was quite pleased with herself.

He didn't seem to hear her. He looked at the document, then back at her intently. His frown deepened. "And Fred would never be party to a plan like this, no matter how good the prank was."

"You think my cat door is a prank," she said, and she could hear the dullness creeping into her own voice. "I think it would be a good idea for you to leave now."

He looked at her sharply, his gaze too all-seeing.

Was that pity she saw crowding the male arrogance

out of his handsome features? She got up, nearly knocking over her teacup. She folded her arms over her chest and then released one just long enough to point at the door.

"Get out of my house," she ordered.

He swore softly—a word only a barbarian would use—got up and moved toward her. He towered over her, and she knew if she moved one inch, he would think he had succeeded in intimidating her.

"Are you telling me this is for real?" he demanded.

"I am insulted that you would think this was anything but real," she said. She heard the hurt in her voice and tried to cover it by pointing at the door once more, more forcefully than the last time.

"You're insulted?" He took a deep breath, looked away from her, ran a hand through his hair and then looked back. "Okay, Bridget, it looks like I made a mistake. I thought the guys hired you to play a prank on me."

"Was that an apology?" she asked. "If so, I seem to have missed the *I'm sorry* part."

Her breath caught in her throat. The man was looking at her lips! As if he found her aggravating and unreasonable and knew of only one way to solve that difficulty!

Well, he probably did only know one way. These types of men had limited methods of communication. Though he did have amazing lips, now that she was focused in that direction. The top one was a firm, hard line, but the bottom one was full and puffy. He wouldn't dare kiss her!

But if he did, she wondered what it would taste like. Feel like.

"Get out," she ordered again, but she could hear a despicable weakness in her own voice, and apparently he could, too, because he made no move toward the door.

Instead he folded his arms over the enormousness of his chest and gazed down at her, aggravated.

"Just for the record, you aren't the only one who got insulted here. Lady, I have built whole houses on a handshake. I am not signing a twelve-page contract to build you a stupid cat door."

"Stupid?" she said huffily.

"Yeah, stupid," he said.

"Fine," she said stiffly. "I wouldn't offer you this job if you were the last man on earth. I will find someone to build my door who has enough integrity that signing a contract doesn't frighten them. And who doesn't think my project is stupid! And who doesn't think I'm an eccentric old—"

"Okay," he said, mercifully preventing her from having to say it—that she was an old maid. "Nice meeting you. Have a nice life."

He went to move by her and then paused, sending a wary glance at the couch to see if his work clothes had marked it. Bridget actually felt a treacherous softening for him when he looked relieved to see they had not. He edged his way to the door.

"Look," he said, an infuriating note of protectiveness in his voice, as if he was the big, strong guy and she was the frail, feeble woman. "Be careful."

"Of?" She tapped her foot and looked at her watch.

"Anyone who needs those kind of instructions for such a minor piece of work is going to be nothing but trouble."

"I'll judge that for myself, thank you."

"I'm just telling you this because Fred would prob-ably kill me if I didn't."

"I am eternally in your debt," she said, but he missed the sarcasm entirely and kept on talking.

"You can buy a cat door at the local hardware. If someone charges you more than fifty bucks to install it, they're cheating you."

"I don't want the kind from the hardware," she said tightly.

"Why the hell not? They're not R28, but I'm sure they work fine."

She debated telling him the truth. She did not want to, and yet the words just slipped out of her mouth. "Conan might get stuck."

She felt an instant sense of having betrayed her cat.

Justin turned and studied Conan. "Why do I get the feeling if that cat was any bigger and I was any smaller, he'd have me for supper tonight?"

He doesn't like you. He's a good judge of character. But she retained any dignity she had left by not saying it.

"Okay, so you want a custom cat door. No more than a hundred and fifty bucks. The fence is the bigger job. I wouldn't pay more than fifteen hundred for it, in-cluding materials. Two thousand if it's cedar."

She felt good manners entailed she should say thank you, but she didn't.

The thought evaporated instantly when he spoke again anyway.

"And don't show that SOW-COW thing to anyone. No self-respecting contractor will want to work for you. It makes you look like a nitpicking perfectionist."

A nitpicking perfectionist? That was at least as hurt-ful as being called Four-Eyes. Miss Priss. A brainiac. Old maid.

"And let me warn you, there are plenty of contract-ors out there who aren't the least self-respecting. Crooks, who would milk a girl like you for all you had."

"I did a lot of research to prepare that document," she said with all her dignity. "And I'm not a girl."

"I'm telling you that SOW COW spells one thing—T-R-O-U-B-L-E." He looked her over, put his hand on the doorknob and then grinned at her with seducing and wicked charm. "And so do you," he said.

Then he was gone.

Bridget snapped the front door closed behind Mr. West and then turned her back and leaned her full weight against it as if she had just narrowly es-caped…well, something.

She wasn't quite sure what.

Or maybe she was.

Though she firmly ordered herself not to, Bridget drifted over to her front window and peeked around the edge of the curtain.

She watched as he leaped into a truck that she prob-ably would have needed a stepladder to get into.

Despite her firm orders to her mind not to think about his body, she remembered it in sharp detail: him sitting on her couch, the large muscle in his forearm jumping every time he took a sip of tea, his jeans molded over the ridged muscles of his thighs, his chest huge and solid under a stained T-shirt. He had probably done that on purpose, made those muscles leap, the swine.

"Well, who is swooning over the swine?" she demanded of herself. The truck started with a roar and pulled away from the curb in a spray of gravel.

He would do everything too fast. A blush heated her neck and her cheeks as her mind flew with that one. "I just meant," she told herself sternly, "that Justin West is a man of rough edges and no refinement whatsoever."

He had insulted her and treated her like an idiot.

"I'll show him," she told Conan. "You wait and see."

Conan opened an eye and regarded her, looking unconvinced.

But Bridget went right to the phone book and made a list of every contractor in the county. In the morning she would check them out with the Better Business Bureau. Within a week she would have a cat door, and Justin West would be a faint, unpleasant memory.

Only that wasn't quite how it worked.

Because a week later she was no closer to getting Conan his cat door. After submitting her prospectus by fax or courier to over a dozen contractors, she had been laughed at, sworn at and hung up on.

Even when she reluctantly retired her SOW, no one had the time to do such a small job. The one quote she was given seemed outrageous, and it didn't even include an automatic cat-door opener. She was reluctantly grateful that Justin had given her a guideline for the pricing of her project.

To make matters worse, Conan seemed to be getting fatter. How could he be gaining weight? She was only putting out a limited amount of the diet food, and he barely seemed to be touching that. She could see the poor cat was depressed. She now saw he *needed* to be outside.

"Oh, Conan," she said, touching his head. "The hair will grow back where the bandages tore it off. And you lost a whole two ounces this week. I'm sure of it."

The cat seemed to know she was lying, just as her inner self knew it was totally untrue that she had not found Justin West just about the most maddeningly attractive man she had ever met.

The house was in darkness and Conan lay sprawled on Miss Daisy's favorite green Victorian armchair, relishing the amount of orange hair he was successfully grinding into the fabric. Some things were off-limits even to him—this chair and the countertops to name a few—but he considered his trespass a legitimate part of his ongoing protest campaign. As soon as he was certain she was asleep, he would make his nightly raid.

Meanwhile he contemplated how life had deteriorated from the dieting doldrums to just plain hell. Starving wasn't good enough. Oh, no, now he had to be bald, too. The bandage removal from his head had taken huge patches of his head fur with it. It was an absolute assault on his dignity.

As if coping with the diet and hair loss were not bad enough, Conan could feel the most subtle shiver in the air since that nasty nail pounder had made his appearance to discuss the cat door. The man had been rather dirty, he'd been rude and he'd been unreasonable to poor Miss Daisy. Still, Justin Pest meant trouble, Conan sensed that as easily as he could sense the coming of a storm. Why else would his fifteen-minute collision with their lives still be creating ripples?

And creating ripples it was! Since that unfortunate

incident, Miss Daisy had not been herself. She seemed constantly agitated, possibly because her attempts to "show him" had been largely unsuccessful. Conan had gotten to the point where he crept into the other room while she did her nightly relay of phone calls to yet more contractors. Her humiliation was painful.

Mostly since it meant she had forgotten on three and a half separate occasions to fill his food dish. Even if it was with diet gruel, the oversight was unnerving. So was the fact that she had been neglecting to scratch his belly on demand and wandering past him as if in a trance, her rumpled list of contractors clutched in one hand.

Judging by Miss Daisy's volatile reaction to the barbaric cat-door contractor, most inexperienced cats would say that Justin Pest didn't stand a chance of worming his way into her life. But cats were equipped with a sonar called instinct, and Conan had *felt* something powerful, perhaps even untamable, in the air between Miss Daisy and the nail pounder. The man did possess a certain powerful ease with himself that a cat had to admire.

History had an unfortunate way of repeating itself, and Conan had lived through this particular scenario before. In his past life, he'd lived satisfactorily with a female of the human species, too. Oh, she had been no Miss Daisy   rather a washout in both the affection and culinary departments, actually—but she had been adequate. She'd opened and closed the door of her trailer home pretty much on demand, kept the litter box reasonably clean and kept the food dish full. Bargain-basement cat food, but at least not diet.

Then some canine-reeking slob had begun to make appearances. And then he had moved in. Before Conan had really adjusted to that, along came that nasty, smelly, screaming baby. And out went the cat.

"Babies and cats don't mix," his previous owner had told him as she'd tossed him from the car into a dark, filthy alley. "Cats have a history of smothering babies, so you have to go."

Of course, this statement was totally unfounded. Conan blamed that particular vicious rumor on those witch-hunting activists four hundred years ago. They had actually published a falsified drawing of a cat sucking the life out of a baby. Human history was rife with wackos! Not to mention barbarians.

Needless to say, although Miss Daisy's reaction to Justin Pest had seemed void of potential for the type of relationship that created yucky, stinky little humans, there was something about her behavior Conan found disturbing.

Among a cat's many, many strong points was superior intuition. And Conan's intuition had gone on red alert when Justin Pest had entered the room. It was not like Miss Daisy to be so fidgety. And what had he glimpsed in her eyes every time her gaze had locked onto one of that man's many bulging muscles? *Hunger.*

Ah, yes, and Conan had become an expert on hunger.

Still, he could sense a very dangerous energy between the two. Miss Daisy had not been alone in sneaking peeks. Unless he was very much mistaken, Conan suspected Justin had liked her kneecaps. And more!

They were just a little too aware of each other in *that*

way. Of course, it manifested as sparks, words spoken with a little too much heat.

Defense mechanisms. Thankfully Miss Daisy's defense mechanisms could rival those around Fort Knox. Hopefully they would protect a poor little cat who had already been abandoned once due to the inconveniences of human love.

It was really too depressing to think about, so Conan lifted his head off his paws and listened. Silence. The house was at rest.

He slithered from the chair and made his way on silent feet to the kitchen. Miss Daisy was in such a state of mind, she was not aware of the enormous butter consumption her household was suddenly suffering.

She had carefully weighted the fridge door with sauce bottles and such so that Conan could no longer open it himself. She had also hidden his nondiet treats and food. Even the diet ration was stored in an inaccessible cupboard above the fridge.

Well, if she was determined to make him resemble a POW rather than a beloved pet, he was called to action. It was not enough to just sulk angrily, especially since she seemed somewhat oblivious to his moods this week.

With all her cat-food-hiding precautions, Miss Daisy had somehow overlooked the fact that she kept the butter on the counter.

Each night Conan delightedly helped himself, making sure to keep the half-pound portions in a reasonably square shape. However, in Miss Daisy's recent state of mind, he doubted that she would have noticed if the butter looked like Swiss cheese in the morning. But the risk of losing his source of saturates produced caution.

He had just had his first lick when he heard a sound. He catapulted from the counter just as the kitchen light was flipped on.

She padded out in her housecoat and slippers. He looked at her, all wide-eyed innocence, not that she seemed to notice.

"It's too late to phone," she mumbled to herself.

Not for pizza, it isn't. Conan rubbed himself against her legs. She reached down absently and petted him and then retrieved a package of graham wafers from the cupboard.

"Not that he looked like the type that would go to bed early. Did he?"

Oh, God. Conan did not even have to ask who.

"Naturally I wouldn't hire him after how he behaved—"

Good.

"—but Fred says he's the best in town. Very fast. His work is apparently impeccable." She sank down on a chair and buttered a cracker. She popped the whole thing in her mouth and swallowed. Conan had the ugly feeling she hadn't even tasted it.

"I said I wouldn't hire him if he were the last man on earth," she reminded herself.

Exactly, Conan thought, *and a better decision you have never made.*

"He is the last man on earth," she wailed, unfolding her list of contractors and studying the crossed-out names bleakly. She picked up the phone.

Drastic measures were called for! Conan leaped on the counter and buried his face in the butter.

"Conaann!"

He hadn't heard such genuine distress since he had launched himself at the window. His face covered in butter, he leaped from the counter and raced down the hall.

After a full second he realized she was not following. He crept back down to the kitchen and peered around the corner at her.

The butter would be stored now, under lock and key, just like everything else. He had gambled with his last card in hopes of distracting her and he had failed utterly. Because she had the phone in her hand and a look of fierce determination on her face.

"My cat is acting bizarre," she muttered, obviously working up her courage and her conviction.

Bizarre? Excuse me? Who was forgetting to fill the food dishes?

"Conan needs a cat door." She drummed her fingers on the tabletop, unaware that Conan had crept back and was watching her.

"Mr. West?" she said. "I'm sorry. Did I wake you? It's Bridget Daisy here." She tucked the phone under her ear and scraped the butter into the garbage. She closed the lid with a snap. "We need to talk about the cat door."

But Conan was sadly aware that whatever transpired between Bridget and Justin Pest next, the cat door was only an excuse.

Still, he had lost the battle—and the butter—but not the war. Surely he was a crafty enough cat that he could get rid of this new threat to his and Miss Daisy's world? That world was topsy-turvy enough with the whole diet thing, never mind adding the complication of a barbarian.

If he played his cards right, Conan thought there was a possibility he might get his cat door first before dispatching the barbarian.

Who needed butter when the world was full of purple finches?

It had been a bad week. Conan had been starved, he was bald and now he had been unfairly labeled bizarre. Still, all cats had been blessed with a gift that the great philosophers and spiritual leaders of the ages tried, largely unsuccessfully, to emulate.

No one could detach from their difficulties and immerse themselves in the pure joy of the moment quite like a cat. Conan lifted his paw to his face and removed some of the lovely pale yellow substance that clung there. He licked it delicately and sighed with bliss.

Ah, Foothills. His favorite creamery.

Chapter Three

Justin folded his arms behind his head and stared up at his bedroom ceiling. He'd called Bridget Daisy "trouble" right to her face, and she'd still come begging, which probably meant she was double trouble.

Not, he decided, that you could call what had just transpired between them "begging." No, dear Miss Daisy had told him how it was going to be, right down to the price she was going to pay—two thousand one hundred and fifty dollars for a custom cat door and a new cedar fence, including materials and labor—and when she expected work to commence.

First thing tomorrow morning, as if he didn't have a house nearly at lockup and three other homeowners breathing down his neck.

A saner man would have just said no. But he already knew every other contractor in town had said just that.

Except for Duncan Miller, who'd said he'd do the job for nine grand.

"I bet I'd earn every penny of it, too," Duncan had told the other contractors who generally gathered for early-morning breakfast at the Roundup Grill and Flapjack House on Main Street.

Oh, yeah, Miss Bridget Daisy had been the talk of the morning-contractor crowd for a week now. They poked fun at her mercilessly. Several copies of her SOW and COW were in circulation.

Justin didn't join in the fun. For one thing, he was at a disadvantage. He was the only one who had actually seen her. The rest of her contacts had been by phone or fax or courier. So all those guys poking fun at the eccentric old-maid librarian really didn't have a clue.

And Justin didn't enlighten them. He didn't tell them she wasn't old and she wasn't ugly. He didn't correct them when they guessed that her panty hose bagged around her ankles and that she bought her dresses in extra-large at Wilson Brothers Tent and Awning.

When the guys painted imaginary pictures of her with granny glasses, pinched face and pursed lips, Justin didn't say one word about eyes a shade of green that haunted him every night before he slept. Or about copper-colored hair that looked as if it needed to be freed from that bun, needed to have a man's hands hauled through it.

Justin told himself his failure to join in the funfest being provided by the circulating cat-door contract and prospectus was only out of loyalty to Fred. Who wasn't actually speaking to him and who had not spoken to him since he had mentioned that his meeting with Bridget Daisy had not gone well.

"Yeer tellin' me," Fred had said sourly, "that a big fella like you was sceered of her waving a few pieces of paper at yar? Poor girl. She must have been taken advantage of afore to be workin' so hard at protectin' herself."

Justin had not wanted to think about it in that light. But he had anyway. He'd thought of that every time another contractor sat down at the Roundup and entertained anyone who would listen with a tale of her call about her cat door. They made fun of what they called her "snooty New England accent." The *sow* and *cow* jokes were flying hard and heavy, with new ones created all the time. They conjectured about her looks and put warts on her nose. They wondered about the exact nature of her relationship with the cat, figuring she was probably casting spells at midnight.

Justin alone knew that with those eyes she didn't have to wait until midnight to cast a spell or need the cat either.

Justin told himself he hadn't joined in because he had better things to do than poke fun at the town librarian. It bothered him that he saw men he had worked with and joked with and eaten breakfast with and drunk beer with in a new light—as if they were small and mean-spirited and didn't have nearly enough to keep them busy.

He felt he could probably attribute this high road of thinking to Fred, but he knew that wasn't the whole truth.

The whole truth was he hardly knew the woman and

already their acquaintance was forcing him to be a better man. Justin hated them laughing at a woman who was misguided but not mean or vicious. She wasn't even that strange. She just didn't know anything about their world and how it worked. Was that a crime?

The whole truth was that Justin wished she wasn't scared of being vulnerable, and after seeing the lunkheads having such fun at her expense, he understood perfectly well why she was.

And now, staring at his ceiling, he told himself he was going to do the job because of Fred, but he knew in his heart of hearts that wasn't the entire truth either.

There was just something about Miss Daisy that was driving him crazy.

In that moment of vulnerability, shaken by sleep as he had been by the husky loveliness of her voice, he admitted what it was.

He wanted to see her again.

Ached for it.

"Trouble," he said out loud. "Justin West, she means trouble."

He was the wrong kind of man to deal with a woman like her. He was all rough edges, and she was all polished refinement. He had learned almost everything he knew about life—and he figured that was plenty—from the school of hard knocks. She came from an ivory tower. What she knew about the real world he could probably put into a thimble. And what he knew about her world—of books and culture and all that crap—could fit in the same size container.

"Hey, West," he told himself sternly. "You're going to build her a cat door. You're not proposing marriage."

Oh, yeah, she'd be that kind of woman. The kind who liked commitment and rings and church bells and everything done just so. He could tell by the way she kept her house and treated her cat. She was just dying to get her hands on something worth caring about.

At least he knew for sure that was not him.

He liked putting his feet on the coffee table and eating supper right from the can. He liked fishing and hunting and a game of pool with the guys. He liked satellite TV because he could watch football and baseball and hockey until the cows came home. And he liked women who wore tank tops and low-slung jeans, who drank too much beer and sang rowdy songs in the parking lot after the bar closed.

But if that was true, how come not one of those women's eyes had ever haunted him long after he'd said goodbye?

He looked at the clock. He should call Bridget back and tell her he'd changed his mind. He'd checked his schedule, he couldn't do it.

This was already way more complicated than he liked his life, and he hadn't even started the job yet.

Of course, if he did tell her the deal was off, then he'd have to explain it to Fred.

And the truth was, he missed Fred. They had talked on a more or less daily basis for a whole lot of years. Fred was what he had left of family. The old guy was solid as a rock, loyal and wise.

And Fred liked Bridget Daisy.

"Okay," Justin bargained with the ceiling. "I'm doing the job. I'll do most of it while she's at work. It will be like my good deed for the year. There won't be any more thoughts of her eyes or her lips or hands in her hair. Not a single one. I will be a perfect gentleman."

There was only one problem. He wasn't quite sure how to be a perfect gentleman.

"I'll bet she'd lend me a book from her library," he said.

He pumped the pillow several times, put it under his head, then over his head, under his feet, then under his knees.

The more tired he got, the more he thought of her eyes and her lips and then he remembered those cute little knees.

Justin West groaned and wondered if he was ever going to sleep again.

He slept in the next morning, which was good. It gave him the perfect excuse not to go to the Roundup for breakfast. Unfortunately, because the Roundup was his daily habit, his own cupboards were dismally short on breakfast fixings. He found a solitary can of tuna fish, which he used to throw together a few sandwiches for lunch. He debated having one for breakfast and decided to take his chances. He'd told Miss Daisy he'd be there first thing in the morning. Maybe she'd have breakfast for him.

Cheered by that thought, he drove to her house. He went through the back this time and surveyed the yard. He'd underestimated its size, which would teach him to get so bewitched by eyes that he forgot to take out his measuring tape before he started tossing out prices.

"Yoo-hoo, Mr. West."

He turned and looked at her. He thought they'd gotten past the Mr. West thing and he was not sure he had ever actually heard anyone use the phrase *yoo-hoo* before.

Bridget Daisy was standing on her small back stoop in a dark flowered dress that looked very similar to the one his eighty-three-year-old aunt Ethel had been buried in.

How was she managing to make that getup look sexy? He supposed, analyzing carefully, trying to force his rational mind to react to her, it was because her feet were shoeless. And her hair was free. And a little breeze was pressing the fabric into her soft swells, and every now and then the hem flipped up just enough for him to glimpse those delectable knees.

"Would you like breakfast?" she called.

His stomach growled appreciatively. He was relieved they were on the same page. He nodded, and she ducked back in the house. He followed her.

The back door led directly into her kitchen, a room at least as disconcerting as her living room had been.

She held the cat back with her foot while he came through the door. The cat looked thwarted. If it was possible, the poor animal looked even more miserable than the last time Justin had seem him. Large patches of hair were missing from his head, pink hide showing through.

Justin was careful not to touch him as he made his way into the kitchen, just in case he had a disease. The cat, naturally, seemed to sense his wanting to keep his distance and attached itself to Justin like a burr to a wool sock, rubbing relentlessly and purring with what Justin interpreted as a certain maliciousness.

"Have a seat," Bridget invited.

Hadn't they been here before?

Where did she find all this tiny furniture? She had a fussy table in a nook just off the kitchen. It was covered with a bright checked tablecloth, and that was covered with a layer of lace. He recognized the teapot and the dainty cups. Also on the table was a tub of plain yogurt, a dish of seeds and a dish of nuts.

He had the horrible feeling that was breakfast.

"Help yourself," she confirmed. "I thought of making you bacon and eggs, but I couldn't really. Conan is on a diet. It seemed unfair to him."

Justin glared at the cat and gingerly pulled back a flimsy-looking chair. He sat down carefully. Could he feel the metal bowing under his weight or was that his imagination? The cat leaped, and Justin grunted at the unexpected weight dropping on his lap. He was sure he felt the chair give a little more.

The feline did need a diet, though Justin hardly thought it was fair that *he* had to suffer because of it. The cat fixed him with mean green eyes, and his purr sounded suspiciously like a growl. They exchanged looks of deep and mutual dislike.

"He likes you," Bridget cooed.

"That's nice." Justin didn't think it was nice at all. He gave the cat a subtle little shove that meant *Get off me,* but the cat settled in deeper, like a wrestler determined not to be toppled.

She brought over a platter of fresh fruit and set it down. Justin noticed the color in her cheeks was high and she seemed nervous.

Afraid, just as Fred had said.

She took a seat. "I wasn't sure if he did, after last time, but now I can plainly see he does."

"Sorry?" he said.

"The cat. I wasn't sure if he liked you last time."

Justin decided in the name of good manners that he wouldn't tell Bridget he didn't give a damn whether her cat liked him or not. He was sure she was reading the signs wrong anyway. The cat's malevolence seemed to deepen when Justin put some yogurt in a tiny bowl, dribbled a little maple syrup over it and began to eat. He tried not to be too obvious in looking around her kitchen for some evidence of a main course.

"So," she said way too brightly, "tell me your plan of attack."

"I thought I'd install the cat door first," he said. "The fencing material won't arrive until later this morning."

"But what if Conan gets out before the fence is up?"

He pictured the fat, bald cat squished under a car. It was not an unhappy thought. Maybe he'd leave the door open on purpose....

He looked at Bridget and sighed. He couldn't do that to her. Her devotion to that wretched cat was obvious. He'd known even the most casual relationship with her would require more of him.

"You can keep the cat door locked until the fence is done."

"Oh, it has a lock," she said, pleased. "May I see your plan?"

"A blueprint? For a cat door?"

For a moment she looked mulish and then she sighed. "Never mind. Fred said to trust you, and so I will."

"Well, thanks so much."

She missed the sarcasm. "Fred said you're a nice man, despite some of the, er, mishaps of your youth."

"Did he go into details?" he asked. Funny, Fred had been letting her know he was a nice guy, when to Justin's face Fred had given disapproving silence only.

"A few," she said with a secretive smile.

This was totally unfair that she had some of the goods on him and he had none on her.

He looked at the dress. Then again, it was perfectly evident there would be none to have on her.

"Well," she said brightly after taking three nibbles of yogurt and a bite out of an apple. "I must go to work. I have to do my hair."

He looked at her hair. It hung in a luscious wave to her shoulders, and the morning sun coming in the kitchen window spun it to gold. "You should leave it down."

Just like that, the tension crackled in the air between them.

The cat kneaded his knee, open claw, and Justin gave him a subtle swat.

"Oh," she said, flustered, "it wouldn't look very good at work, would it?"

"It looks great here. Why wouldn't it look good at work?"

"It doesn't seem professional to leave it down," she said, but her voice held uncertainty.

And then, as if he wasn't playing with fire, he leaned over and touched her hair. It felt exactly as he had known it would, as soft and silky—

The cat kneaded a little farther up.

Justin launched from the table, knocking over his teacup with a clatter. The cat leaped free and squalled indignantly as it hit the floor. The tea spread in a dark ring over the lace. The cup was lying on its side but thankfully unbroken.

"Sorry," he said. He turned and glared at the cat. It slunk away, but not before he caught a look of pleased satisfaction.

"No, it's perfectly all right, really." She was up and clearing things from the table. He got a cloth from the sink. Moments later she whisked off the tablecloth and lace. Breakfast, such as it was, was over.

"The cat clawed me." He sponged tea off the floor.

"What? Where?"

"My knee," he lied.

"Oh. He's never done that. I'm terribly sorry. Do you want me to put on some antiseptic?"

"No, thanks." His voice croaked. He'd said it quickly enough that she knew it wasn't his knee.

A deep rose blush moved up her neck to her cheeks. He wondered if it moved down, too. It was enough to make him forget the growling in his stomach.

"Oh," she cried and looked at her watch. "I'm late for work."

He had not been to the library since he had struggled though his grade-twelve history project, but back then it had opened at ten.

He said nothing, though, watching her scurry about, endearingly flustered.

The soiled table coverings went in a small washer near the back door. The machine looked as if it was big enough to hold one pair of his socks and a T-shirt. The laundry seen to, she gathered up her purse and tried to jam her feet into the wrong shoes. She left, ran back a few minutes later and plucked her keys off a hook by the back door.

"Do you need a house key?" she asked. "I like it locked if you need to go anywhere."

"No. I'm not going anywhere."

That came out sounding all wrong. As if he would wait until the sun set forever in the sea, if need be, for her to come home.

"I usually come home at lunch," she said, "to visit the cat."

"I'll see you then."

She blushed as though he had asked her to the prom.

"I can make you something for lunch."

God forbid. He might starve to death. "I brought some, thanks."

"All right, then." She flew out the door as if she was a deer with hounds on her heels.

He noticed her hair was down. And he really didn't know if that was a good thing or a bad thing.

He was on his knees inspecting the door and taking his first measurement when she opened it again, into his head. He fell back and grabbed his head. His hand came away red.

"Oh, I'm so sorry." She was on her knees beside him, her hand on his brow.

This job was turning out to be dangerous in more ways than he'd imagined.

"It's bleeding," she reported. He suspected her matter-of-fact tone cost her great effort. Her skin had become so pale, her freckles stood out endearingly. He covered the wound with his hand, but she pried his fingers away.

"Let me look," she ordered courageously even though it was obvious to him she did not want to look.

"I'll get my first-aid kit," she said after a moment and clamped his hand back down over his wound. "And an ice pack."

"Hey, it's a scratch. A long, long way from the heart. Go to work." The truth was, even if it was a twelve-inch gash that was life threatening, he didn't want Miss Daisy working on it. Her hand on his forehead made him feel as if he had crossed a desert and was dying when this cool, soft touch had been laid on his head, a miracle of hope and tenderness. If one touch could do that, he wasn't undergoing the entire first-aid treatment. Plus, he had seen the cat's bandaged head the first time he had been here. No, thanks.

"Go to work," he said again, gruffly. *Please.*

She stood up and regarded him uncertainly for a moment and then nodded. "All right. Yes. Work. I think you are right. It's barely a scratch. It's stopped bleeding."

"Great."

"All right. Goodbye." She smiled, and he was that man dying of thirst in the desert again, and her smile was a drink of water, sweet and life-giving.

"Goodbye," he said firmly.

Bridget was halfway to work before she noticed her hair was down. And that was after she had run the stop sign on Tenth and Main

She reviewed her morning so far, and not with pleasure. She had gone back to tell Justin to be very careful not to let the cat out while he worked around the door. But when she had hit him in the head, she had totally forgotten what she had gone back for.

Now she couldn't remember—had she told him or not? She was flustered. That man flustered her. She had been flustered from the moment she had seen him, the light dancing in those amazing gold-green eyes, and everything had just gotten worse when he had reached across the breakfast table and touched her hair. What on earth had he meant, touching her hair like that?

They were strangers! It was totally inappropriate.

She should have told him so.

Oh, no. Not only had she not said a word, she had leaned toward him, caught his fragrance, swayed....

She nearly ran over the little old lady who was pushing one of those wire boxes on wheels. The woman looked to be doing her civic duty—picking up small pieces of rubbish and clutter from the streets.

A terrible thought blasted through Bridget's brain: *That could be me in my old age. Eccentric. Alone. Faintly pathetic.*

It occurred to her for perhaps the first time in her life that she did not want to grow old alone.

"That's why you have Conan," Bridget reminded herself.

But the sad truth was that Conan at his very, very best had never once made her feel the way she had just felt when Justin had reached out and touched her hair.

Not cool and collected and in control like her normal self at all.

No, Bridget had felt like a woman. Feminine, mysterious, powerful, on fire with life, as if her whole existence suddenly had potential for things it never had before.

Adventure. Romance.

And then, when she had touched his head where that trickle of blood came out, her fingertips had tingled after she'd pulled them away.

She had seen something in his eyes that had made her breath stop in her throat. What had it been? She sorted through words like a computer searching the thesaurus.

And suddenly she came up with exactly the right one.

Longing.

"You are reading far too much into a tiny encounter," she said and pulled into her parking spot. She hit her Reserved sign so hard, it bent over on its metal rod. She blushed and backed up.

The man had her in a state.

She couldn't go home for lunch. She was a hazard.

"You don't have to wait until you get old. You're already pathetic," she said to herself, getting out of her car and carefully locking the doors.

A man had touched her hair and she was twisted in knots. She had touched his forehead and it was making her act as if she'd had three glasses of champagne for breakfast instead of yogurt.

Still, she knew it would be a mistake to go home at lunchtime.

Thankfully Conan, her built-in excuse, was expecting her. She had never let him down before and she wasn't about to start now.

But Bridget Daisy knew, as she unlocked her library door, that the tingle she felt in her tummy had nothing to do with going home to Conan.

Chapter Four

The cougar's cold, off-yellow eyes narrowed on its unsuspecting prey. His claws rhythmically contracted and retracted, his tail swished in silent, delicious anticipation. Every muscle in his sleek two-hundred-and-twenty-six-pound body tensed into a death crouch, ready to spring, ready to sink his claws into warm flesh....

A cough—purely human—snapped Conan from his Discovery Channel reenactment. Dejectedly he shrank back to his wholesome twenty-six pounds, and the cougar's honey-brown fur melted back to his own burnt-orange. Perched on the countertop, not on the limb of a tree, Conan glared balefully at the man on his hands and knees in front of the back door.

The man was a problem. Conan was forced to admit that thinking he could get his cat door *and* eliminate that problem had been just plain wishful. That was evident from the disgusting display of out-of-control chemistry over breakfast this morning.

Miss Daisy and Pest were two very different elements, but when combined, they could make one hell of an explosion. Conan didn't like explosions. Thus he labeled the situation CODE RED. Justin Pest had to go…before lunch, if at all possible.

Pest, of course, had no idea how lucky he was that Conan was not large enough to give this problem an edible solution.

Still, Conan fixed the broadness of those shoulders with his finest, most intimidating predator-to-prey stare. A purr of pure pride escaped him as the human shifted uncomfortably, glanced over his shoulder and then glanced over it again.

"Don't even think it," Pest growled with not even the slightest pretense of friendliness now that Miss Daisy was not here to impress. Conan realized, annoyed, the man was not going to be anything or anybody's prey. Even a cougar probably would think it over, move on to something smaller and milder.

So how to get rid of this threat to Conan's rather cozy arrangement with Miss Daisy? Trying to play Mr. Pest had too many dangerous elements, something like trying to play with a Rottweiler.

Physical attack was out of the question.

Still, Conan knew himself to be brilliant, sophisticated and cunning. He *had* to keep these two crazy humans away from each other.

Conan stewed fervently from his countertop perch, all the while pretending to be supervising the cat-door progress. After almost half an hour of deliberation, the plan that came to him was stunning in its simplicity and near diabolical cleverness.

Why, he would use Miss Daisy's devotion to his own precious self to nix things before they got going. What could turn off the surging energy between the two humans faster than Miss Daisy getting really, really angry? And what would make Miss Daisy very, very, see-red angry? The loss of her precious Conan, of course! The loss of her precious Conan due to the nasty nail pounder's carelessness!

Conan grinned devilishly and studied Justin Pest more closely. He was precisely the kind of man who didn't understand subtleties. Miss Daisy had neglected to instruct him precisely about her cat's safety. But even if she had, you could tell by the set of his chin and the knit of his brow that he wouldn't be letting any wisp of a woman tell him what to do.

Pest should be guarding that door as if his very life depended on it. But he wasn't, and that wisp of a woman wouldn't accept that kind of disrespect from a mere barbarian.

"That's it," Conan announced to himself. "I am running away." He chuckled as he pictured Miss Daisy's fury directed at Pest when she discovered her cat missing. After a breach of trust of that magnitude, Pest would be yesterday's news.

Conan felt a deep purr of contentment begin to sing within him as he contemplated the finer points of his plan. Running away, albeit temporarily, would be a masterstroke, multifaceted in its advantages and consequences.

Not only would Miss Daisy be furious at Pest for his

carelessness, but by the time Conan returned to the fold, doing his best to look half-starved and street-rumpled, Miss Daisy would be so happy to see him and so shaken up by his ordeal that she would completely forget her ludicrous diet ideas. Guilt and giddy happiness at his return would translate into anchovy-topped pizza, shrimp, ice cream....

A string of thick drool trailed from his mouth and landed on the floor with a wet plop. Pest turned and gave him a disgusted look, which he met with his most innocent expression. Now all he had to do was wait for the perfect opportunity, and nobody could outwait a cat. He folded his paws underneath his chest, curled his tail around himself and closed his eyes. He may have actually drifted, but a slight sound alerted him to opportunity.

He opened one eye, a slit that would have made a cougar proud. Justin Pest, with one quick glance Conan's way, went out the door and down the outside steps, clumping the "all clear" noisily.

He had carelessly pulled the door behind him, but Conan had not heard the snap of the latch catching. He unfolded himself from his position, stretched luxuriously and hopped off the counter. He snagged the edge and the door swung open. The moment almost seemed too simple, too easy, too unheralded. Conan waited, listened, then sighed with pleasure. He waltzed right out that door, pleased that the escape required very little effort or physical exertion.

He went in search of the human. Pest was sitting on the tailgate of his truck, wolfing down a sandwich, reading a plan and jotting down numbers. Conan sat in the shade of a honeysuckle and waited for Justin to spot him. It was a weakness, but he wanted to relish Pest's panic-stricken expression before he made his escape complete.

Pest, unfortunately, seemed engrossed in the plan.

After waiting an annoyingly long time, Conan meowed.

Pest looked up. "I thought you weren't supposed to be outside until the fence was done."

Uh, your responsibility.

Pest rolled up the plan. "I guess when a guy's gotta go, he's gotta go, huh?"

Ugh. Too bad Miss Daisy hadn't been around for that one. The man's vulgarity and crudeness were really much worse than she could have imagined.

Still, Conan couldn't help feeling a bit disappointed. He'd expected to be chased, to make some bold and wily cat maneuvers, maybe go up a tree. Instead Pest strode by him as if he were nothing—*nothing*—and went back to work.

Conan thrust his nose into the air and marched toward the street. Obviously, as well as being coarse and vulgar, the man had no clue of the severity of the situation he had just created, no idea of the depth of Miss Daisy's devotion to her favorite feline friend.

Nice knowin' ya, Mr. Pest. He strutted down the sidewalk. Freedom and fresh air felt wonderful, intoxicating. He'd visit the birdbath at the park first. And then maybe he'd head downtown. The trash can behind the Roundup Grill was a taste treat almost beyond belief.

"The diet is done," he sang to himself. "Done, done, done."

And then he stopped in his tracks, arrested by a heavenly scent.

Tuna? Was it possible? His nose led him right to Pest's big truck. With great effort, Conan launched himself upward, caught the open tailgate with the tips of his paws and hauled himself up.

A cooler that obviously served as the world's largest lunch bucket was there, the lid slightly askew, the aroma wafting out of it absolutely delectable.

The birdbath at the park would just have to wait. Besides, he liked the idea of eating Pest's lunch *and* getting him into doo-doo with Miss Daisy.

Conan stood on his hind legs, front paws latched onto the edge of the cooler. He looked in through the crack in the lid. The sandwiches lay just beyond paw reach. He batted the lid open a bit more and with a great sigh Conan hefted himself over the top—just as in the old war movies. He found himself in the narrow, dark confines of the lunch container. It was a tight squeeze, but he still expertly snagged a sandwich from its plastic wrapper. He dispatched the top slice of bread, admired the chunky white of the tuna momentarily and then dug in with an appetite that would have done his relative, the cougar, proud.

His diet-starved brain and body were consumed in the flavor, the sensation, the texture of all that tuna....

Too late, he heard an approaching whistle. He went very still. Then, without any warning at all, the lid of the lunch bucket slammed shut and there was only darkness.

He pondered this development briefly, then thanked his lucky stars that he was a cat, and cats knew how to make the most of each moment.

After all, there were two sandwiches left to go.

* * *

The opening for the cat door was framed in. He'd install the actual door when she got home so she could see the cat use it the first time. Justin had the feeling she'd like that small, thoughtful gesture. He hadn't seen the cat for a while, but he didn't mind that. Being stared at while he worked this morning had made the hair on the back of his neck stand up. As ridiculous as it seemed, that pudgy puss, with his slitted eyes and swishing tail, had actually reminded Justin uncomfortably of a cougar he had watched the night before on the Discovery Channel.

Meanwhile, Justin had started ripping down the pieces of leaning old fence when Bridget Daisy drove back up. He watched her get out of her car, a nondescript gray sedan exactly suitable for a librarian. She shot a little look his way, was flustered to have been caught sending a little look his way and leaned back into the car.

It gave him a fascinating look at the soft roundness of her rear end. She came back out of the car, her arms loaded with books. Why would she bring books home on her lunch hour?

She was flaky as hell, he told himself, hoping to knock back some of the purely masculine awareness her cute little rear had caused in him. She probably read to her cat. She came into the yard and surveyed his work, peering studiously over her stack of books.

He wondered if they were a defense mechanism, something for poor, shy, flaky Miss Daisy to hide behind.

It didn't work. Sometime during the morning she

had found the time to put her hair up, but a strand or two had worked loose, and she kept blowing them out of her eye, since her hands were full. She'd also had time to get a run in her stocking, just above one of those little knees that he liked so much.

"You've done quite a lot," she said, her voice faintly strangled. She surveyed the knocked-down fence briefly, but her eyes kept skittering back to his bare chest. He had stripped off his shirt over an hour ago.

"It's coming okay," he said, closing his fist over his hammer and curling his arm slightly. It was all he could do not to grin at how her eyes widened at the leaping muscle in his forearm and biceps.

She ducked her head and gripped her pile of books tighter to her chest. Her voice even more strangled, she said, "I always come home at noon. To be with Conan."

Making sure he didn't think she was coming home to be with him, slanted looks at his chest and arms not withstanding.

"Yeah," he said dryly. "You said that already."

"I did?"

"This morning."

"Oh. Well, then, I'll just go in and see Conan."

It was quite fun making her flustered. And it really took so little effort. "Um, I think he's wandering around out here somewhere."

Bridget went very still.

"Out here?" she asked, aghast. "Mr. West, I specifically asked you not to let him out. Didn't I?"

He stared at her. She had? Her eyes were bewitching. Somewhere between the cat clawing his privates and his stomach rumbling over the disappointment of the breakfast she'd provided and being clunked on the head hard enough to see stars and the mystery of her eyes, he must have missed that.

No point admitting it, though. "I don't think you did."

"Even if I didn't say it *specifically,* you must have known! Why would I be going to all this trouble to build a fence if the cat roamed free like some neighborhood pest?"

She wasn't looking flustered now. Unless he was mistaken, that pink tinge in her cheeks had nothing to do with her awareness of how the sweat was sliding down the column of his throat.

"How is it," she asked, her voice rising, "you can remember I told you I'd be coming home for lunch, but you can't remember I specifically told you the cat was not allowed out?"

"You just said you may not have been that specific," he pointed out. Her coming home for lunch had interested him, and nothing about that mangy slit-eyed cougar-impersonating cat did, not that it would do at all to tell her that. Especially not now, with her ruffling up her feathers like an indignant chicken

His fascination with toying with her aside, he *hated* that tone of voice. It was the schoolmarm-to-dunce voice, and he'd been on the receiving end of that just a little too often in his painful school years.

He put down his hammer, picked up his shirt and dried the sweat off his chest with it, well aware of the look in her eyes—battling to stay annoyed, distinctly distracted. He slipped the shirt over his head, but slowly.

She licked her lips.

If he worded this right, he wasn't even going to be in trouble. The cat would probably be disappointed by that.

"There's probably no nice way to say this," he said. It was kind of one of those the-dog-ate-my-homework moments that he remembered so well from his school days.

She went pale. "Has something happened to my cat?"

"No, no," he assured her hastily, taken aback by the very real fear that flashed through her eyes. "Nothing like that. But he got out a while ago and he had that look about him."

"What look?" she asked, wide-eyed.

"Like he had to take a crap," he confided in her, leaning a little closer. Too late he realized it might have been wiser to word that more delicately. How would you word that for a librarian? *A call of nature?* Lordy, she'd be a hard woman to be around. A man would always have to be on his toes, thinking of ways to word things delicately.

Luckily for him he had no plans to be around her. And from the look on her face, that was probably a good thing.

Because the little librarian nearly lost her grip on her books in her haste to reel back from him. Her facial expression could have flash-frozen a fish.

"He has a litter box for that," she informed him icily. "In the basement."

"Are you telling me your cat shi—answers calls of nature in the house? That is gross."

Her bottom lip quivered, and he didn't think it was

because she wanted to laugh either. She said stiffly, "This is a new low. A barbarian calling *me* gross."

"A barbarian?" he said softly. Oh, he wanted nothing more at the moment than to be a complete barbarian. He'd like to take those prissy little lips underneath his own and kiss her until the last thing on her mind was her stupid cat. Those books would be scattered at her feet and she wouldn't even notice....

She must have seen it all in his face, because when he took a step toward her, she backed hastily away. Her heel caught, and the books did go every which way.

"Oh!" she said. "These books are brand-new!"

"Hey! I didn't drop your stupid books."

The look she gave him was killing. "Books are not stupid."

"Oh, right. Barbarians are stupid," he muttered. He crouched down beside her and helped her retrieve the books. His knee, unfortunately, brushed hers.

Damn, that made things complicated. Because he'd let her cat out, and she'd called him a barbarian, and he'd called her books stupid, and he wanted nothing more in the whole world than to place his big hand over the tininess of her knee and just see what happened next.

Her books gathered up, she gave him another fish-freezing look and flounced into the house.

Moments later, with no books, she was out looking under every shrub and up every tree, calling Conan over and over again in a forlorn, desperate voice.

"Look," he told her finally, "there's no such thing as a cat that comes when it's called."

She gave him a frosty look, but he saw the desperation in it and he made an awkward effort to comfort her, even though he owed her absolutely nothing after that "barbarian" remark.

"He'll come back. Cats are like bad women. You can't get rid of them."

"You don't strike me as any kind of expert on cats. Bad women, I'm sure, are a totally different story."

He could see temper flashing in her eyes, but he could feel a little of his own temper growing.

"Look, Miss Priss—"

"Miss Priss?" she gasped. "Oh, I hate being called that!"

Meaning she'd been called it before, and for good reason, too, he was willing to bet, even though he felt an illogical fury at whoever had done it.

"Miss Daisy," he amended, his tone infinitely reasonable. "I'm doing you a favor by being here. I don't need a piddly little job like this. But I'm here to put in a door and build a fence, not to babysit a cat. Nowhere in the SOW/COW did it mention babysitting a cat."

"In case you haven't noticed, the cat you're building those things for is no longer in need of them, since he's missing. Thanks to you."

"Maybe you should have locked him in the bathroom if you were so worried about him."

"I thought I could trust you."

"Your mistake," he said with a shrug. No, he was not a man a woman like her could trust, and he didn't mean about her cat either. He couldn't be trusted to word things delicately and he had designs on her knee-caps that would shock the hell out of her if she ever found out.

Which she was never going to.

"I think our relationship is over," she said.

Their *relationship?* Sheesh.

"I haven't even blown in your ear," he said and was rewarded by the deep stain of crimson that flooded her delicate little features.

"Mr. West, go away."

"Are you telling me I'm fired?" he asked, not even trying to keep the hopefulness from his tone.

"That's exactly what I'm telling you! I wouldn't let you touch another thing on my place if you were the last man on earth."

"Yeah, well, I've heard that before."

"It was my mistake to take it back."

"No, it was mine for letting you take it back!"

They glared at each other for a moment. Then she turned on her heel, went into her house and slammed the door. Unfortunately it was no longer even faintly soundproof since there was a large hole in the bottom of it.

Unless he was mistaken—and he was pretty sure he was not—she burst into tears the minute that door was closed.

See? He could not be trusted with a woman of such delicate sensibilities and cute knees. Should he go tell her he was sorry? About what? The cat? He wouldn't even be able to pretend he was sincere about that!

Justin decided he hated that cat more than he had ever hated anything, including his grandmother's home-made sauerkraut. If he ever saw him again, he was going to do himself, Miss Daisy and the world a big, big favor.

Muttering to himself, he gathered up his tools. He did it slowly, because he was hoping she would notice that big hole in her door—big enough for skunks, raccoons and other vermin to get through—and that she would come out and beg him to fix it before he left.

He would refuse her! Unless she was crying. Then he wasn't quite sure what he would do.

The door of the house opened. He crossed his arms over his chest, narrowed his eyes, stood with his legs apart, his most intimidating stance, a man not moved by tears. His extra hammer flew through the air, and he had to abandon his intimidating stance to avoid being hit. It barely missed him and landed with a thud at his feet. The door closed again.

He stared at the hammer with real consternation. Who would have thought she'd have that kind of throwing arm?

He picked it up, shoved it in the loop in his apron, threw stuff in the back of his truck and took off with a surprising display of temper, considering how he wanted to look cool and unconcerned about what had just transpired at the home of Miss Bridget Daisy.

Damn her.

And her cat.

And her stupid door.

And her nylons with a run in them. And her lips. And the way her hair had turned to copper in the sun. And the way he had seen the passion flash like a promise in her green eyes when she had lost her temper.

And damn the fact he was probably going to have to go back and fix the hole in her door. Not finish installing the cat door, mind you. No, nothing like that. Just fix the hole in the door so he wouldn't have to lie awake at night worrying about skinny thieves, rapists or other pint-size ne'er-do-wells getting into her house.

He got out of the truck at his house. He'd been unaware he was going home until he arrived there. He had a pile of work to do, but the sad fact of the matter was that he had never felt less like doing it. He scooped his lunch kit from the back of the truck and went through the front door into his own house, which was unlocked despite his brand-new awareness of all the lurking dangers in Hunter's Corner.

He set his lunch box down in his front entryway and glanced into his living room. Unlike her, he lived in a newer section of Hunter's Corner. His house was modern and bright. He wanted to feel reassured by the order, by the clean lines, by the large, leather, masculine furniture and the plasma-screen TV that took up nearly an entire wall of his living space. Instead he was resentfully aware that his house seemed faintly sterile, unwelcoming.

"At least," he muttered, "none of the furniture will collapse when you sit in it."

Beer, cold and frothy, was calling his name. Maybe more than one beer. It was only one o'clock in the afternoon, but when a man was this rattled at this time of day, he had to do what he had to do. Imagine being rattled by that pinch-faced little pipsqueak!

With eyes so green you could practically dive into them. And that mouth that needed so badly to be kissed, and that hair that needed to be loosed—

"Argh!" He leaped back from his lunch kit as if it was possessed. It hadn't moved! Had it moved? Cautiously he reached out and touched it with his toe—and leaped back again when the whole lunch kit lurched toward him, wobbled and then fell over on its side. Beer forgotten, his heart hammering in a way he recognized as most unmanly, he righted the lunch container. It lurched again. He undid the catch, leaned over and jerked back the lid.

Twenty-six pounds of furious fish-reeking orange fur exploded from within and attached itself to Justin's face with fangs and claws. Reeling around his entryway in a terrible two-step, Justin frantically tried to pry the frightened beast from his face. But no sooner would he unhook one paw from his cheek when it would embed itself in his ear or his chin or his nose. Finally in a flurry of self preservation he managed to detach all the cat's feet from his face at the same time. He held the squirming, windmilling body at arm's length just long enough to determine it was indeed the missing troublemaker, and ignoring the shrieks of protest, he crammed it back in the lunch box and slammed the lid. Muffled determined yowls came from inside. Justin duct-taped it shut for extra measure.

Then he sat right on top of it, dabbing at the cuts and scratches on his face with the corner of his T-shirt and contemplating his options. A fast drive to the closest bridge and a quick heave over the side, and all his problems would be over.

"I'll go get her a cute little kitten," he decided. "Or a turtle. A hamster would be nice."

The lunch cooler heaved underneath him. He sighed. The awful truth was that he was going to have to bring the cat back. And fix the hole in the door.

And then it was *adios* to her and her crazy cat. For good. Forever.

Chapter Five

Bridget was vaguely aware that she probably looked dreadfully unprofessional, not the way the town librarian was supposed to look at all. She was supposed to be at work. She had never missed work. The chess club would be lining up outside the doors of her library looking at the Closed for Lunch sign with bewilderment.

But instead of opening the doors of her library, here she was scouring the ditches of Hunter's Corner for her cat. She had never missed work before. Of course, her travesty was such that she hadn't even changed her clothes. As soon as she had heard Justin's truck drive away, she had realized she had no time to be feeling sorry for herself.

At first, she had really thought she was going to find Conan almost immediately. But now, an hour later and a long way from home, with her hair loose and plastered to her forehead by sweat, her heel broken on her shoe, her dress snagged and rumpled and her nylons shredded, she wasn't so sure.

It was disgraceful to be looking this way on the side of a public road. Most people would think it was silly to feel this panicky, this despondent, over the disappearance of a cat.

Of course, it wasn't just a cat. It was Conan. Conan, who purred her to sleep every night and whose substantial weight was such a joy on her lap when she read. Conan, who endlessly entertained with his many adorable snoozing poses and his great passion for cuisine. Conan, for whom she could buy little cat beds and coats and toys. Conan, whom she could go home to every day, instead of to an empty house. Conan *needed* her.

And if it was desperate and pathetic, then it was desperate and pathetic, but she needed him, too.

Guilt about depriving him of his favorite foods stabbed at her, a knife to her tender heart.

And she wouldn't be in this position if it wasn't for Justin West! How could he be so careless, so insensitive, with what meant the most to her? Why had she trusted him?

Didn't she, of all people, know the dangers of trusting? She had been a little girl, only five, when her father—a big, laughing Black Irishman who had been her whole world—had walked away from her and her mother and never looked back.

Her mother had seemed afraid of men after that, mistrusting, and Bridget had understood her fear perfectly. She had also understood, at some level, she could keep her own fear at bay with a perfectly controlled world where no mistakes were allowed.

Mistakes somehow had come to include most of the masculine race, with their treacherous and unknowable hearts. Bridget berated herself now. She should have taken one look at Justin's boyish grin and nauseatingly handsome features and known to lock her cat in the bathroom and her heart in ice!

Her world was being turned upside down and given a good shake because of that horrid man, with all his rippling muscles and self-assurance, his easy lady-killing hazel eyes, his *sweat* trickling down his jawline in the most fascinating way.

"Revolting," she said out loud. But it wasn't. It was disorienting and drugging. Even now, with her precious cat gone, what was she thinking of?

Him. Not Conan. Justin.

"Conan," she called, her sense of mission renewed. "Conan, please." She scanned the ditch, pausing to listen for the distraught mews of a lost or wounded cat.

Her heart stopped. In the ditch ahead of her was something ghastly and gray. Even in her sheltered world she understood it was something very dead, smooshed beyond description or recognition.

Her cat was not gray—but what if he was covered in mud? What if his insides were outside? What if he was maimed beyond her ability to recognize him?

She took a deep breath. "Courage," she ordered herself sternly. She scanned the ground and found a stick. She moved forward, hesitated and closed her eyes. She took another deep breath, which was a mistake. Bugs swarmed her. She opened her eyes and prodded the corpse. She thought it was possible she was going to faint, and she was no closer to knowing if that grotesque *thing* was her beloved Conan.

A huge vehicle pulled up beside the ditch and stopped. She could see the tires. She tilted her head, recognized the vehicle and looked around for a place to hide.

He could not see her like this, prodding dead things, her hair in disarray, her clothing ripped, on the verge of hysteria.

The door swung open. He surveyed her grimly, as if trying to decide if it was really her. He must have concluded it was.

"Get in," he snapped.

A shiver went up and down her spine. He could be quite masterful, not that she'd ever let him know that. And she had never wanted to be rescued more in her life, not that she would ever want him to know that either. She lifted her chin and scowled sternly—her perfect miffed-librarian look. She hoped she looked dignified and unapproachable and that the fact she was shaking was not showing.

She was not getting in that truck! Not if her very life depended on—

"I found your cat."

Her eyes skittered to the gray blob pasted to the end of her stick and she hastily dropped it. She saw suddenly that the blob was what was left of some poor raccoon. It was not her beloved cat.

That determined, she couldn't get away from the decaying raccoon fast enough, and she scrambled up the side of the bank and contemplated Justin's truck. There was going to be absolutely no ladylike way to get into that vehicle. While she contemplated her options, a strong hand emerged out the open passenger door, wrapped around her wrist and yanked.

With a very unladylike plop, Bridget found herself sitting on the passenger seat of Justin West's truck.

It was as she might have imagined it would be. There was mud on the rubber floor mats, building plans crammed untidily onto the center seat, the ashtray was full of nails. She was sitting on the edge of a metal builder's square and she moved slightly so it wasn't poking her quite so intimately. She took it all in, anything to avoid looking at him.

"You look like a bag lady," he said after a moment.

Even though it only confirmed what she already suspected, it felt like a brand-new low. She had just been called a bag lady by a barbarian.

"Thank you," she said, primly folding her hands in her lap. "I know that. I was just so focused on finding Conan." She remembered why she was sitting there. Shock washed over her. Her cat might be dead, maimed, injured, and she was taking in every detail of Justin's truck and trying not to be carried away by how his aroma was so strong in there.

"Is he all right?" she asked in a small voice. "If he's dead, you can tell me." Her voice caught.

"I regret to inform you he's alive and kicking," Justin said dryly. "Make that scratching."

She hazarded a look at him for the first time and gasped her dismay. His face was crisscrossed with deep, painful-looking scratches. Unfortunately each scratch seemed to highlight perfect, mesmerizingly masculine bone structure.

"What did you do?" she managed to squeak. She had a sudden and completely insane desire to touch his face, as if her hands could soothe away some of the pain she saw there.

She tucked her hands firmly under her thighs.

"What did *I* do?" he shot back, indignant.

She could not give in to the tenderness that tugged at her. If she did, it felt as if she would be lost, as if she would fall into a world as foreign to her as the surface of Mars. A world of heightened awareness, of hearts that beat too hard, of glances that caught and held, of yearning for…well, all kinds of things that the prim town librarian did not yearn for. A world that required trust. A world so new that she would make mistakes, and probably lots of them.

"Well, Conan wouldn't just attack you for no reason!" There. That sounded so much better, so much more in control than. *You poor baby. Let me make that all better for you.*

Bridget blushed at the very thought. She was not the kind of woman who knew how to make things all better for a full-grown, red-blooded man. She had a first-aid kit at the library and occasionally dispatched a Band-Aid and a kiss to the under-five crowd. But this was a totally, totally different experience.

"Well, he did. He attacked me for no reason. I opened the lid of my lunch container, and he exploded out of it and attached himself to my face."

"He was in your lunch container? My poor baby." But only she knew which of her poor babies she was referring to.

Good grief. As if the six-foot-something of pure

bristling male energy on the truck seat beside her was going to be anybody's "poor baby."

"Your poor baby?" His voice was rough with aggravation. "Your poor baby ate my entire lunch! I think I may have been attacked for the sole reason that he ran out of tuna fish sandwiches."

Conan did love tuna fish. But enough to attack a man over it? Surely not! Rather than admit her doubt, she said, "I don't understand how he came to be in your lunch cooler."

"He tricked me into thinking he was having a bathroom break and headed for my lunch, I guess. I must have accidentally slammed the lid on him, maybe when I left your place in such a hurry."

It was insinuated but not said that if she had not made such a fuss, he would not have left in such a rush and the cat would never have gone missing in the first place. She was not quite sure what to make of a man who thought a cat could trick him.

Obviously she should not be charmed by it.

But for a reason she could not begin to comprehend, she was.

"The important thing," she said with a sigh of pure relief, "is that Conan is safe."

"Unfortunately he is, though I might have rated the important thing as a visit to the hospital for me."

"None of those need stitches, do they?" That required another long look at his face. Could someone really be born with such a perfect chin? Whiskers were darkening on it. She sat harder on her treacherous hands.

"I wasn't thinking stitches. I was thinking rabies. Tetanus. Penicillin."

"My cat's shots are entirely up-to-date. And he's an extremely clean animal."

"Whatever," Justin said with just enough cutting disbelief to almost entirely erase the attractions of his nearly perfect chin. Almost.

Bridget, eyeing his strong profile, suddenly realized that Justin did not look like a man who would *want* to return a cat that had just mauled him and generally caused him nothing but grief. If he was a true barbarian, he probably wouldn't have. He probably would have taken her cat and—she shuddered just thinking of the possibilities—dropped him off the edge of a cliff or used him for skeet practice. A true barbarian would have a thousand unsavory ways of disposing of a bothersome cat.

But he hadn't. So she reluctantly forgave him for calling her a bag lady, for questioning the cleanliness of her cat and for making her *feel* as tumultuous and off balance as if she had just ridden a roller coaster.

Bridget said with as much grace and dignity as she could muster, "Mr. West, thank you for bringing him back."

He nodded grimly.

"You must have dropped him at my house? And noticed I wasn't there? And come in search of me? Really, that is all very sweet."

He did not like being called "sweet." She could tell by the tension that rippled through his shoulders, briefly knotting the exquisite muscle of a large forearm and ending with his huge fists tightening a little more on the steering wheel.

"That's me," he said dryly. "Mr. Sweet. Though your

cat might not agree. I didn't drop him off at your place. I haven't been there yet."

"But then where is Conan?"

He jerked his head and she looked out the back window of his truck. In the box was the lunch cooler, wrapped in duct tape. As she watched, it jiggled like a Mexican jumping bean.

She had to bite back her desire to scream at Justin to stop the truck. Conan trapped in the barbarian's lunch box?

As calmly as she could she said, "He will be frightened in there. If we could just stop, I'll put him on my lap—"

"Now you're frightening me," he said. "I am not sharing the cab of my truck with that cat."

"You don't look like much would frighten you," she said. No, he certainly did not look like a man easily frightened. She could imagine him standing up to a charging grizzly bear!

"Looks can be deceiving," he said. "The cat stays right where he is until I get you home. It's only a few minutes."

She could hardly be unreasonable after all he'd done—and not done—to her cat. She shot Justin another look and could not help but notice the rather stubborn cast of that rather glorious chin. She realized he was in no mood to be taking suggestions from her. Conan was going to have to wait. They were only minutes from her house. Surely that wouldn't traumatize her poor cat too much?

She realized she was being asked to be a bigger person than she wanted to be. Because instead of focusing on what she wanted and on her cat, she needed to express how sorry she was that Justin had been injured and for the events leading up to his injury.

"Mr. West," she said, "I want to apologize. I'm very sorry you were attacked by Conan. He must have been very frightened and disoriented when you opened your lunch box. He is generally a very loving animal."

Justin snorted, but she went on with determination. "And I must admit that I may have overreacted when my cat went missing. There was certainly no need for name-calling. I shouldn't have fired you. You were absolutely correct. I did not hire you to babysit my cat."

He looked straight ahead, stone-faced.

Somehow it suddenly seemed very important to her that he understand this. She was not a quack. She was not an eccentric old maid.

"It's just that—" The quiver in her voice took her by surprise, and she paused and regained her composure. "It's just that Conan is all I have."

"You aren't going to cry, are you?" He glared at her with very real horror, and she saw that some things were far more frightening to him than charging grizzlies.

"No, I'm not," she said with dignity and then swiped at her eyes. She had managed to make herself look pathetic after all.

Conan is all I have. She would have done anything to grab those words back.

"I mean, of course he isn't all I have," she said into the terrible quiet that now filled the cab of the truck as they both contemplated the pathetic emptiness of her life. "I love my job. Adore it. And my house is great. It was built in 1932...."

Her voice trailed away before she embarrassed herself any further.

He glanced at her and grunted, but his stern facial expression had softened somewhat. Probably for all the wrong reasons.

The last thing she wanted from a man like Justin West was his pity. Thankfully he pulled up in front of her house and slammed on the brakes before she could do any more damage. Given more dead air between them, she would probably start waxing poetic about the chess club and the plaster detail in her 1932 home.

Without waiting for her, Justin was out of the truck. She had a fantastic thought: what if a gentleman hid inside that rough exterior after all? What if he had so hastily exited the truck so he could open her door for her, help her off the huge drop from truck door to sidewalk?

She waited, then glanced over her shoulder. Justin was lifting the lunch cooler from the back of his truck with easy strength. He hoisted it onto his broad shoulder and moved down her walkway. Thankfully he did not even appear to notice she was still sitting in the truck! And just as thankfully he did not witness her awkward attempts to get out of his truck by herself and keep her skirt in a decent place as she slid down onto the sidewalk.

She limped up the walk after him on her broken heel, cursing his broad back and his easy strength and his lack of manners and trying very hard not to notice the way those faded jeans clung to his behind.

"You should really keep this locked," he snapped at her when he opened her back door.

"I was upset."

"That's exactly the opportunity criminals look for."

Just when she had almost talked herself into believing he was just about the worst heathen she had ever met—magnificent behind aside—he went and spoiled it all by worrying about her!

He set down his container with just a bit of a bang, and Bridget heard an indignant cat cry from within. She sprang forward, but a strong arm wrapped around her waist and held her. She felt the breath leave her in a whoosh. All those muscles had warned her he would be strong, but nothing in her limited experience had prepared her for what that strength would *feel* like.

He released her almost instantly. "Be very careful," he warned her.

"Conan would never hurt me!"

He looked dubious, but as it turned out, springing the cat was not a quick process anyway. Bridget had to retrieve a pair of scissors and cut away the duct tape. The cat moaned piteously the entire time, and the cooler jiggled sadly, as if poor Conan's energy was waning.

She glanced at Justin to see if he was noting these signs of Conan weakening, but his arms were folded across his chest and he was glaring at the lid of that lunch box, his expression warlike. Ready.

Ready to protect her.

It was kind of sweet, even if it was ridiculous. Conan would never hurt her. The jiggling within suddenly stopped, and Bridget slid open the lid of the cooler. Conan was prostrate within it, his eyes wide and unblinking.

"Ohmygosh," she said softly. "I think he's dead."

"He's not dead," Justin said firmly. "He's pretending to be dead. To get me in trouble."

Really! It was the second time Justin had attached a rather conniving motive to a pure, simple animal. What kind of man did that?

A warrior. Never let his guard down. She almost sighed with a kind of primitive appreciation.

But then Conan meowed weakly and blinked at her once, very slowly, reminding her she had a traumatized cat to deal with! This was no time to be daydreaming about warriors.

Bridget put her hands tenderly under the cat's limp form and with an unladylike grunt of exertion lifted him from the lunch box.

"Oh," she said. "You poor sweetheart." She kissed him and hugged him close to her.

The cat mewed weakly again, and she tucked him close to her breast. He closed his eyes, nestled deeper, and after a long moment, Conan began to purr with deep and utter contentment. His familiar warmth seeped into her, and she would have enjoyed the moment immensely except for the fact the warrior was watching her with narrowed eyes. And one other small fact.

She laughed out loud. "My gosh, Conan, you are aromatic!"

"Aromatic," Justin repeated. "That's a fancy word for *stink*, right?"

"Right," she laughed. "What is that smell?"

"Tuna. He ate the parts of my lunch that he liked and rolled in the rest of it."

She could forgive him that tone of voice. And look at his poor face! She could forgive him his dislike of the cat.

Reluctantly she put Conan down.

"Mr. West, I just don't know how to thank you."

"Never mind," he said gruffly. He turned and eyed the door. "I'll get this fixed up for you so you don't have to worry about the cat getting out. Or the bogeyman getting in."

The cat wandered crookedly over to Justin and rubbed its head vigorously against his shin.

"See?" she said. "He must have just been frightened when he attacked you! I can tell he really likes you."

The cat threw up on Justin's work boots. Bridget's eyes widened. Who would have guessed a cat, even quite a portly one, could hold that much food?

"Yeah, I can plainly see that," Justin said.

"I'll get a rag. And I'll make it up to you. I've behaved terribly—I was distraught. Would you like to stay for dinner?"

Her timing was terrible! Who mentioned dinner within seconds of a cat vomiting? Her timing had always been terrible around men. Especially goodlooking, self-possessed ones like him. She felt awkward and gauche and like a complete idiot.

"Of course you don't want to stay for supper!" she said swiping away at his shoe. "Of course you don't!"

And she didn't want to trust him and she certainly didn't want to make mistakes.

He reached down and took the rag from her, shoved her gently out of the way and cleaned the mess off his own shoes.

"Sure," he said. "I'll stay for supper. But don't cook," he added hastily. "You've had a heck of a day. We'll just order pizza."

Justin's eyes, more gold than green, held her eyes

steadily, and she had the craziest thought she'd had all day. Maybe in her entire life.

She thought, *Maybe I can trust this man.* She thought, *Maybe it's okay to make mistakes when you are learning something new.*

Conan, apparently now completely recovered from his ordeal, did a complete ecstatic circle, flopped down on the floor and waved all four paws in the air.

The taste was electrifying, completely intoxicating. Tuna, expertly mixed with a hint of butter and mayonnaise. So rich, so plentiful. And then…slam! Heaven gone, and in its place complete and utter darkness. A roaring noise and then a horrifying journey, being tossed, turned, tumbled in that small space. Bread, spit-dampened and now devoid of tuna, was being mashed into precious fur.

He could tell that the prison had become mobile and he suspected the ugly truth. He'd been kidnapped by the Pest. Conan realized he hadn't been subtle enough in his hostility. His threat had been recognized. And now, destination: unknown. He was probably going to be tossed off the edge of the earth. Or worse, thrown into a dog kennel.

Conan, full of fear and tuna, was swept with nausea. He heroically fought down the urge to vomit. The bread sticking to his fur was indignity enough.

He tried to be philosophical. If he was going to die, wasn't it great that he was going to go with a belly full of tuna?

The short answer? NO!

He was not going to die. He tried to reassure him-

self of that fact with a life count on his claws, but this only led to more hysteria when he couldn't decide definitely on a number. Which of his nine lives was he on anyway? Did cracking his head open on the window count as one life? It hadn't been that close, not really. Still, wouldn't that have been eight? If it counted?

What a fool he had been to underestimate Pest! The man had realized their goals were the same.

They both wanted Miss Daisy to themselves!

It was a well-thought-out kidnapping. The back door left artfully open, the tuna bait, the stealthy approach before the slamming of that lid.

What now? What end did that murderous man have planned for the small feline obstacle positioned between him and the librarian?

The truck stopped and the engine died. His container was being lifted, and Conan just knew it was going to be opened right into the jaws of a rabid Doberman or the spill gates of a dam. Could he hear water running? A dog panting? Oh, God, he was sure he could. He would not faint! No!

He braced himself for a heroic last stand, ready to launch himself from the tuna-tainted prison and give his assailants a last fight that they'd never forget....

The doorbell of Bridget's cozy little house rang just as in his dream the lid to his box sprang open. Befuddled, still caught in the tangle of the nightmare he'd survived, Conan catapulted from his leather chair and landed a little too solidly on the smooth hardwood floor. He skittered wildly across the glossy surface, collided with the throw rug and mercifully gained traction before he hit the delivery boy and toppled the pizza.

"Nutty cat," the kid said.

Don't tip him, Conan thought, but of course the Pest tipped him.

"Yeah, he's crazy," Pest agreed before he shut the door.

Conan fixed him with a stare. He was not crazy. He happened to be suffering from post-traumatic stress disorder. And though it was true Pest had returned him home, Conan was not at all sure the whole episode had not been a warning.

The man might be diabolically clever, though he certainly didn't look it. It would not do to underestimate him again. But certainly all wars had to have a cease-fire declared for important occasions like Christmas, peace talks and pizza deliveries. So with all the dignity he could muster Conan trailed the man carrying the pizza into the kitchen, where Bridget was setting the table.

He went to his favorite spot underneath her chair and savored the fact that despite his horrible adventure, he was now safe and sound at home.

If his nose was not mistaken—and of course his nose rarely was—the pizza was the meat-lover's special. Bridget reached under the chair and scratched his belly with such affection that he just knew the immediate future was secure.

Sure enough, she popped a large chunk of cheese-encrusted pepperoni in front of him.

"Let's forget the diet for tonight," she suggested.

He was all for forgetting the diet for all time, but for now he was just going to be content that he was alive and actually eating pizza, something dead cats did not do. Tonight, later, he was going to have to figure out what life he was on.

If he'd used them all up, he might have to forget the war on Pest. After all, maybe the guy wasn't so bad.

Maybe he'd taken him by accident.

He'd returned him, hadn't he?

And weren't they all here together, eating pizza, just like one happy family?

"I wouldn't give him too much pizza," Justin said. "He just got sick a little while ago."

Okay, buddy, Conan thought. *I hope you enjoyed the truce while it lasted.* He glared at Justin's big toe, thinking how when he wriggled it, it looked surprisingly like a mouse. Why would anyone wear socks that were gray and shedding hair?

Really, no one would blame a guy for attacking a foot disguised in such a deliberately misleading way. Add to that several other facts: Conan was hungry, had lost his lunch and was now being deprived of his rightful share of pizza.

Still, he had to think things all the way through. Cat society could be unforgiving, and human toes were well documented to be disgusting bacterial breeding grounds, suspected of causing felines disease and other unpleasantries.

Conan glanced over at Miss Daisy's petite little toes tucked within her spotlessly clean socks. Surely not all human toes, just—he shot a disdainful look back to Justin's feet—the majority.

Besides, he still had that life thing to figure out, and it was a good guess Justin would not react with gentle forbearance to a full-out attack on his feet.

No, like any brilliant strategist, Conan would have to bide his time, wait for his next opportunity to dispose of the barbarian. Meanwhile, there was his delightful Miss Daisy's finger under the table with a nice little nibble of bacon attached to it.

She didn't even miss a beat in the conversation!

Chapter Six

The cat under the table was making Justin nervous. He was sure the beast was eyeing his toes!

But he would do well not to forget the real threat was not Conan the Fat Cat. No. The real threat was sitting across the table from him, eating her pizza daintily with a knife and fork.

Miss Bridget Daisy a threat? It was laughable, really. She was prim and proper and faintly frail-looking, not the kind of woman who threatened a man at all. She had changed out of her torn librarian dress and was now wearing cream-colored slacks that were not tight in any of the right places and a blouse that wasn't either. The blouse was a horrible shade of lavender.

There were no sexy sideways looks. The blouse was buttoned firmly to the very top button. There were no tosses of that shimmering mane of pure copper. And there certainly was no coquettish blinking of those amazing green eyes.

Bridget Daisy could probably win a contest: the Least Threatening Woman in Hunter's Corner. But that was the trick. She looked so unlike anything a guy had to worry about that she just kind of slipped in under a man's guard.

That's why he was sitting here sharing pizza with her, when he'd been so determined to fix her door and go home. To say goodbye to her and her cat for good. He had used the word *forever.*

He felt a breath on his toe and yanked his foot under his chair. He glared under the table. The cat smirked at him from beneath Bridget's chair.

She was feeding it a glob of cheese off her finger.

Another surprise attack from the understated Miss Bridget. Because suddenly Justin wondered what her fingers would taste like if a man kissed them, took the clean, slender tips of them between his teeth and nibbled....

"Uh," he said hurriedly, trying to force his wayward mind in any direction but the one it was determined to take. He looked up from under the table and into the brilliant green of her eyes. "How come you bring books home?"

"Pardon?"

Jeez. Just say *what* like everyone else.

He nodded at the leaning stack of books on her counter. "I noticed you brought those home at lunch. Do you bring work home often?"

"Oh." A delicate blush crept up the ivory of her skin, the kind of blush that should really be reserved for much more momentous events.

Like the suggestion of a kiss.

Good Lord, for Hunter's Corner's Least Threatening Woman, she sure had gorgeous lips. Full and plump. If she licked them right now, he was probably going to do something really dumb. Like leap across the table and taste them. And her fingers, too, while he was at it. If he was burning his bridges, he might as well plant a little kiss on those kneecaps, too. He wondered how prim Miss Daisy would react to that.

Maybe she was right. He *was* just a barbarian. He certainly had never wanted to be one more than he did at this moment.

Thankfully she did not lick her lips. She lifted her linen napkin to them and dabbed.

"I don't have to bring the books home," she said shyly. "They came in this morning, brand-new."

She looked at him expectantly, as if he was supposed to decipher this statement.

She interpreted his baffled look, and her blush deepened. "I just love new books," she confessed in a husky voice. "I love the way they look and smell. I love the way they feel."

Was she doing this deliberately? Torturing him with that sexy voice, making him wish it was *him* she wanted to look at, smell and feel?

"There's nothing quite like running the new page of a book through your hands," she said dreamily.

He could think of something. He tossed down his napkin and got up hastily. "You would have hated me as a kid," he said. "Getting my smudgy little hands all over your books."

Her gaze went to his hands. Something white-hot

flashed through her eyes. Did her voice have a faint ragged edge to it when she said, "I am quite protective of my books."

Danger. He had to get out of there. The librarian was an imposter. She was pretending to be the least-threatening woman in Hunter's Corner.

Ha!

He was not sure he'd ever been up against anyone like her.

"Well, I better fix that hole in your door and then be on my way."

"Can I help?"

Of course she couldn't help! She was a librarian who liked the way books smelled. She didn't know anything about masculine stuff, tools and tape measures, saws, hammers. She had written the SOW/COW, proof of her ignorance in matters such as this.

But a treacherous part of him insisted on dancing with her danger instead of running from it.

"You want to learn how to use a cordless drill?"

"Yes!" she said with such real enthusiasm he had to smile.

But he wasn't smiling later, as his hands guided hers on the drill, as they put in the last screws for the cat door. He was way too close to her, but safety dictated he had to be. Her little tongue, pink and plump, was poking out between pearly teeth. An aroma was coming off her that was as sweet as alfalfa allowed to bloom. Her brow was furrowed in intense concentration. The screw went in sideways—again.

He went to show her how to reverse the drill, but she batted his hand away. "I know how to do it!" she said.

"I can clearly see that," he teased.

Oh, a man could get used to teasing a woman like her, a woman who took life and herself a little too seriously, a woman who needed someone to coax a smile out of her.

It came, the smile, like sunshine piercing clouds. And then it was followed by laughter. She reversed the drill, started again. Her laughter was not the laughter of a reserved little librarian. No, it was more robust. The laughter of a woman who wanted very badly to let go and had not had enough opportunities.

It changed everything about her, that laugh. It erased the worry line at her brow and put a light of almost leprechaunlike mischievousness in her eyes. It changed everything about him. It made him want to be the one to make her laugh, over and over again.

The drill whined.

"There," she said with satisfaction and sat back on her haunches to survey her work.

"Great," he said dryly. "Only seven more to go."

A job that would have taken him ten minutes was now going on an hour, and he was not sure when he had ever been so happy about a delay.

She was funny. She was bright. She was sexy. He wasn't quite sure how she was managing to be sexy in a blouse of that color, but the truth was the color was kind of growing on him, just like her. It was a color a person had to look at a bit, a color that intrigued.

Her shoulder brushed his, and he was aware that he liked it. The color of that blouse she was wearing might be odd, but the fabric felt nice, soft and silky. He glanced at it. In fact, it really wasn't that bad after all.

A few more screws and the cat flap was done. She sat right back on the floor and studied it. She pushed it experimentally with her hand and laughed gleefully when it swung outside and then swung back.

"Done?" she asked.

Well, he just about was. He was not sure how much more of her aroma, her closeness, her laughter he could handle without stealing a wee small kiss.

"Uh, don't forget rodent-infestation protection." He held up the weather stripping and showed her how to fasten it, then watched as she did so.

The problem was, how did you steal a kiss from a girl like Bridget? She was deep. She loved the smell of books, not dancing on tabletops after a few too many beers. She wasn't the kind of girl who gave away kisses—or allowed them to be stolen—without some sort of agenda.

A kiss to her wouldn't just be a kiss. No, not that simple. It would be some sort of promise.

Fred thought she'd been hurt, and Justin kept catching glimpses of wariness and then feeling foolishly pleased when something he said or did chased the wariness away.

But that was missing the point! She wasn't his kind of girl. Because he wasn't making any kind of promise to anyone. He was a completely free man for the first time in years and he wasn't surrendering that, especially not to a complicated kind of woman who would probably expect all kinds of things from him that he was not prepared to give.

He slid her a look. She was the kind who would like her car door opened for her and her jacket held. She was refined and educated, and he wasn't. It was that simple. A mule and a thoroughbred did not share the same harness.

It would be a big mistake to take this any further. It had gone as far as he could allow it to go.

Maybe he had already allowed it to go much too far. Why else would the thought that they were incompatible, drastically unsuited for each other, be causing this funny little pain in his heart?

He started gathering up his tools, looking everywhere but at her and her lips.

"Well, that's it," he said way too jovially. "Cat door accomplished. Hey, would you look at the time? I've got to go!"

"Go?" she said, jumping up and brushing off the seat of her pants. "You can't go! We have to test the door."

Right. How could he have forgotten? And what about the fence he had to build? Sheesh, even if he got away this time, he had to come back. And work for the most-threatening woman in Hunter's Corner again.

She seemed absolutely oblivious to his discomfort.

"Conan!" She disappeared into the far reaches of the house, calling for the cat.

"Just hold out a piece of pizza," he suggested under his breath. Another difference between them: he was cynical, she was sweet.

She thought that cat was some kind of noble and lovable creature. She was so darned *ready* to love.

And he wasn't.

He could slip out the door and disappear. He was good at the disappearing act. He'd done it dozens of times down at the old bar and grill when some girl was heating up to him and he wasn't. She went to the ladies' room, he went home. But Bridget wasn't like the girls who hung out down there. She was *tender*. A man could bruise the sensibilities of a woman like her without half trying.

Which just confirmed his earlier position. They were too different. He could probably make a catalogue of their differences that would rival what Sears Roebuck had to offer. He had to get out of there. Before one of them got hurt, and probably her. He could send someone else to work on the fence. There was a kid who had been bugging him for a job....

But as soon as she came back into the room, grunting under the weight of that enormous cat, his plans evaporated.

She looked irresistible lugging that cat around.

She set Conan by the new cat door. She nudged the door with her foot to show him how it worked. The cat glared at the swinging door with pure malice.

"I'll go outside," she decided, "and call him."

"A little bit of pizza might help."

She genuinely looked as if she would have never thought of that on her own. She didn't have a clue how the male mind worked. Not a feline one and not a human one either.

Poor girl.

She fetched a little sack of cat treats and went out the door, closing it behind her. "Conan," she called, lifting the flap a little and showing him the bag of treats, "come through your door."

Conan squatted down like a sumo wrestler who didn't plan to be moved.

"Come on, Conan, your favorite. Tuna."

"Don't remind me," Justin said.

The cat shot him a look of malevolence, and she shook the bag more vigorously.

"Come on, Conan," she pleaded. "Try the door."

The cat, without rising, shuffled his position so that his back was to the door. He buried his head in his paws and closed his eyes.

"I don't think he likes the door," Bridget called plaintively. "Wait! Maybe he's sick of tuna. I'll try turkey." Turkey treats in hand, she tried again. The cat ignored her, the treats and his new door.

Justin had had about enough of Conan for one day. Wary of claws, he picked up the cat and bowled him right through his new opening.

"Good cat," Bridget said on the other side. She fed the cat several of the turkey treats and then passed the bag though the opening.

"Okay, call him through that way."

Justin was not calling a cat!

"Justin?"

"Here, kitty, kitty," he said with unenthusiastic reluctance. But it didn't matter how he called or rattled the bag. The cat would not come back through the door.

After trying for a few minutes, Bridget came back inside, the cat in her arms. "It takes him a while to get used to new things," she said apologetically, setting the cat down.

"Okay. Well, I really have to go."

"Justin?"

"Hmm?"

"Nothing," she said quickly. She studied her toe,

then said in a rush, "Will I see you tomorrow?" He was silent and she hazarded a glance at him. "When you come to build the fence?"

Not if he could help it. "You might have already left for work. I have to stop at the building-supply store before I come over."

"Oh."

Was she disappointed? Well, that's what big, rough guys like him did to refined little things like her. Better to do it now than later. He opened the door, eager to make his getaway.

"'Bye then," he said gruffly.

"'Bye."

And then without warning she reached up on tiptoe and kissed him on the cheek.

It was as tender a sensation as he had ever felt—as if his cheek had been brushed by the inside of a flower, by something so delicate and soft it might evaporate if you tried to touch it or hold it or capture it.

She stepped back. She was blushing wildly, as if she had propositioned him. "Just...thank you, Justin. For the door. For bringing my cat back. For the pizza. For my new cat door. It was fun."

He stared at her. He felt frozen to his spot. He felt he needed to run, but he could not.

Fun. It had been fun. What was it about the plain little librarian that could make the most ordinary of things seem fun? That could make an innocent little kiss like that seem like a doorway to another world? A world he had no interest in, he told himself. Jeez, if he entered that world, before he knew it he'd be calling cats and feeling the pages of new books.

He had just gotten out of a world of caring for some-one else, or being committed and responsible. He wasn't going back there for a long, long time. He'd promised himself that. But his promise felt as weak as if it was written on the gossamer wing of a butterfly.

"There's a poetry reading at the library on Wednes-day night," she said. "If you wanted to come…"

"A poetry reading?" he repeated with astonishment. As if to drive home the fact that he was not entering her world, he stepped hastily out the door he had already opened.

He wasn't going to a poetry reading with her. No, no, no. That would give the wrong message entirely. It would say there was something about her world that in-trigued him. It would say there was a crazy chance that their two very different worlds had a meeting place. It would say this encounter was going to go somewhere beyond building a fence and a cat door.

At his hesitation, her tentative smile disappeared and she seemed to shrink. The lavender blouse looked ugly all over again.

"What was I thinking?" she stammered. "Of course you don't want to go to a poetry reading."

"Yeah," he said. "I mean, anyone could tell I'm not a poetry kind of guy." *At all.*

"Of course," she said. "I'm sorry I just thought—" *Don't ask.* "You just thought what?"

"I just thought maybe you'd think it was fun. In an unexpected way. Like me learning to use the drill was fun."

She was tripping over her words now, trying to re-tain her dignity. He had the awful feeling she might be trying not to cry, which was a stern reminder that she was far too fragile a flower for a big lummox like him.

On the other hand, maybe the reading *could* be fun in an unexpected way. His life suddenly seemed as if it had become altogether too predictable. It held no surprises, few unexpected delights, nothing *new.*

The obvious answer was to take up bungee jumping. Skydiving. Bear hunting. Any of which seemed far less dangerous than her.

"I guess I could go to a poetry reading," he heard himself saying.

"No, no. It was foolish of me to ask. Forget I said anything."

But he could tell he was not going to forget the pain in her eyes for a long, long time unless he did something to make it right.

"No, I insist. I'll come to the poetry reading. But on a condition?"

"That is?" she said with dignity.

"It's your world, Bridget, and if I try it, you have to try mine."

West, what are you doing? the voice of his reason cried out.

He overrode it.

"What do you mean, try yours?" she asked, her voice a whisper of hope and yearning.

"I know a great fishing hole."

Her eyes went very wide. "You want me to go fishing with you?"

The cat yowled and tried to rush out the door Justin was holding open. He shoved the cat—none too gently—back in on the toe of his boot.

"Oh," she said, flustered. "Oh. That would be fine. Fishing."

"All right, then." When it looked as if maybe she was going to kiss him on the cheek again, he closed the door rapidly and headed down the walk.

"Don't forget to lock the cat door," he called back over his shoulder.

It wasn't until he got home that he allowed the full insanity of what he had done to hit him. He'd said yes to going to a poetry reading. A poetry reading. Him. Justin West. And as if that hadn't been damage enough, he'd had to tangle their lives just a little bit further.

Fishing. He was going to take her fishing.

She'd squeal at the worms and stand up in the boat and probably dump them both in the water. Bridget Daisy all wet. Hmm. Maybe this wasn't as crazy as he'd first thought.

Of course it was! He picked up the phone. Fred had gotten him into this mess.

When Fred answered the phone, Justin ignored the sleepy note in the older man's voice and asked without preamble, "What the hell do you wear to a poetry reading?"

And if Fred was the least bit surprised or intrigued by that question, he had the good sense not to let on. "Why, I think a sports jacket and a pair of jeans would be good," he answered.

Bridget leaned on the door long after she had heard the truck drive away. She was shocked at herself.

"I think I have behaved like a complete floozy," she confided in the cat. "Ohmygod, Conan, I kissed him. I

mean, just on the cheek, but really, what was I thinking?"

She forced herself away from the door, grabbed a
broom and began stabbing frantically at the sawdust on
the floor by the door.

"And if that wasn't bad enough, I asked him out! I
don't think, according to Miss Post, I'm supposed to
ask him out."

She moved the sawdust around a little more. Conan
seemed to want more details, and she hoped if she
talked out loud, she could make herself understand this
moment of madness that had overcome her.

"To a poetry reading. I asked Justin West to a poetry
reading. How could I? Justin at a poetry reading. What
was I thinking?" She snorted out loud at the ludicrous-
ness of whatever she had been thinking.

Well, the simple and sad truth of the matter was she
had *not* been thinking—or at least, not straight, not
since the moment he had picked her up from the ditch
this afternoon in that big truck.

No, even before that.

From the very first time he had dominated her fragile furniture with his big frame it was as if her brain
had stopped working correctly. It was determined to
block out all those painful early-childhood lessons
about trust.

Conan meowed and brushed her legs.

She picked him up. "You've had a hard day,
haven't you? I think maybe one little piece of pizza
wouldn't hurt. I just have to make a quick phone call
first."

She set the cat down. Fred's number was busy. At

least he wasn't asleep. She paced restlessly, tried again in a few minutes.

This time the phone rang and he answered.

She made small talk trying to think of a clever way to get to the point. Cleverness evaded her.

"Um, Fred, I was just wondering if you could tell me what a person wears to go fishing?"

If the question, asked at ten at night out of nowhere, dumbfounded him, it did not show in the unchanging calm of his voice.

"Uh-huh," she said. "Oh, I see. It depends on the weather. Of course it does. I knew that! But generally shorts, a light blouse and a hat? And don't forget the sunscreen? And bug spray? Why, Fred, I think I would have forgotten those! Thank you so much!"

After she hung up, she realized Fred had not only not sounded the least surprised by her call but he had also not expressed the tiniest bit of curiosity about who she, the town librarian, was going fishing with.

She went into her bedroom and rifled through her closets. She had shorts, of course, but suddenly they all looked distinctly librarian. Too long, too conservative, not what a person would wear fishing at all.

She tried on the least conservative of the lot, a white pair, above the knee, pleated. She had a matching belt and a solid-colored navy top. She assessed her reflection in her full-length mirror. She looked like a professional woman golfer!

"Not that there is a thing wrong with professional woman golfers," she confided to herself, but then dejectedly slumped onto the bed. It wasn't the image she wanted!

Conan jumped up beside her and whined piteously.

"You poor baby," she said distractedly. "You have had a hard day."

She stopped, frozen. What was she doing trying on shorts? Fishing was sometime in the future, the date as yet unnamed.

The poetry reading was on Wednesday! Two-days-away Wednesday. In very short order, every other item of clothing she had was pulled out of the closet and displayed on the bed.

Her wardrobe, she decided fretfully, was something an old-maid librarian would own.

"I am an old-maid librarian," she wailed.

The cat covered its ears.

She tried on every single dress and pair of slacks she owned. She tried desperately to add some pizzazz to her dismally unsuitable wardrobe with the artful use of colorful scarves and belts.

It didn't work.

She had to have something new. That was all there was to it. A new outfit, sleek and sophisticated.

Colorful.

"Sexy," she said out loud and was both shocked and a little proud of herself.

Conan leaped out from under the bed and playfully attacked her ankle. She shook him off absently, stooped and patted his head. "You're so cute," she said, but her mind was elsewhere.

Could Hunter's Corner provide such an outfit? She thought of the tiny department store on Main Street that smelled of dust and had poor lighting.

Wednesday. She had never missed a day of work.

She couldn't possibly book off, not for something so very frivolous. Somewhere in that pile of unglamorous choices she had a plain black cocktail dress. It was simply going to have to do.

Conan had abandoned the bedroom in disgust and lay sprawled on the kitchen throw rug, his claws clenched deeply into its fibers.

You're so cute, indeed.

He glared at the newly renovated door Pest's towering frame had long since disappeared through. The little ripples of disturbance the carpenter had created in his life were now beginning to resemble a tsunami. What had Pest been thinking, tossing Conan through that cat door as if he were some sort of *object*. Hmph!

The man was obviously defensive of his workmanship and feared rejection in front of Miss Daisy.

Well, inspiring a little fear was okay with Conan. He wasn't going through that door again, not if his life depended on it. Maybe that would help make his message clear to his googly-eyed mistress.

Pest was a mistake!

Though the sickening truth, if that display going on in the bedroom was any indication, was that it might take more than a door boycott to return her attention to where it belonged, which was on her beloved cat.

All through dinner Miss Daisy had been making clumsy attempts to brush her feet with the Pest's, apparently oblivious to the fact Pest's feet were gross! Thankfully Conan had been perfectly positioned to intervene, and she had ended up brushing him. He purred loudly, remembering her stricken, confused expression when she'd peered under the table and found that she was only making contact with her cat. It was more evidence of her addled state that she had expected Justin's feet to be that furry. As humorous as the whole incident had been, Conan had to be very, very careful not to be swept away by amusement in such an obviously dangerous situation.

The danger had been underscored to Conan when Miss Daisy had invited the barbarian to a poetry reading! The event itself was insignificant because, as far as Conan knew, it didn't involve food of any kind. But it was further disturbing evidence her common sense was being thrown to the wind. Couldn't she see it was like inviting an elephant to a ballroom dance class? Pest at a poetry reading simply was not a fit!

Miss Daisy seemed to be forgetting what was important, and that would be the fact that her favorite feline had been recently victimized by that very poetry-reading invitee!

Conan had actually thought she understood the depth of his post-traumatic stress when she had offered him that slice of pizza, but that promise had been made to him almost two hours ago. He decided he'd better go make sure that she hadn't entirely forgotten that important detail amidst the flood of unimportant ones between her and Pest.

Conan found her collapsed on her bed, surrounded by what he suspected to be every piece of clothing she owned. He leaped up beside her.

"Oh, you poor baby, you've had a hard day," she said to him in a soothing tone.

She'd already said that, but he decided to overlook

it. He purred and closed his eyes, practiced the art of telepathy. *Pizza for the cat. Pizza for the cat. Pizza for the cat.* His visual was so clear he began to drool. He relaxed and let his body go limp in anticipation of her picking him up and transporting him to the kitchen.

Several seconds passed, and Conan cracked open one eye. Miss Daisy had gone back to doing whatever she had been doing before he'd arrived!

Irritated, Conan climbed down from the bed and launched a slightly more aggressive warning attack on her ankle than the last time.

"Oh, you're so cute," she muttered distractedly.

Cute was all well and good, but not when there was pizza involved!

"Meow," he cried loudly. Meaning: pizza. Now. He swatted at her ankle again, but she moved deftly out of his way.

"The black is going to have to do," she said unhappily. "I'm going to have to wear this to the poetry reading." Miss Daisy took a drab black dress from one of the piles accumulated on the bed and delicately laid it out on her bed's last clear space.

Conan was astounded! The ugly truth was now completely clear to him. She had totally forgotten about the pizza promise! Miss Daisy was totally immersed in nitpicking over clothing to wear for *him*, the Pest.

Conan watched her with aggravation. Now she was hunched over, sniffing several dusty bottles of perfume that looked as if they were remnants of her high school years. Then she scooped up an armful of makeup, circa the same era, and headed into her bathroom.

Really, she had left him with no choice.

Let this be a lesson to you.

Conan pounced silently onto the black dress and rolled with it onto the floor. He attacked with vigor, thrashing the piece of black material this way and that, covering it with saliva and orange hair.

"Conan!" The rage in her voice stopped him midswipe.

He stared at her as she came back into the room. She had on red lipstick and blue eye shadow. Only on one eye, though. She looked hideous. And she was screeching in a voice that matched her face, "Conan! Now I'll have to get that dry-cleaned. I suppose it smells like fish."

Well, that would be Pest's fault.

She buried her nose in the dress. "Oh my gosh… Conan, why?"

He glared at her with a haughty lack of apology. He'd give her one reason. Pizza. He concentrated very hard. Pizza.

But she did not get the message at all. In fact, Bridget scooped him up, and, considering what a terrible day he'd had, not with the loving sympathy he deserved.

She marched over to her bedroom door.

"Get out." She tossed him out of the room with a regal sniff and shut the door firmly behind her.

He landed with an undignified thump in the hallway and stared at the closed door. Never before had he been denied access to parts of the house.

Depressed and pizza-deprived, Conan slunk back to the throw rug in the kitchen. He eyed his new cat door with hatred. In fact, he decided, he hated the whole concept of human relationships.

But at least in her agitated state Miss Daisy had left out the butter.

Chapter Seven

Justin looked at the worn dry-cleaner's sign. In his line of business, it was not one of the Hunter's Corner establishments that he had to frequent with any regularity. In fact, the last time he had been there had been for Harry Burnside's last wedding, seven years ago. No, make that eight. Harry was single again, another reminder of *why* being there was not the greatest plan.

Relationships complicated the nicest of lives.

Though when Justin tried to come up with what was so nice about his own life, at this moment, he drew a blank. He didn't really have a life. He worked hard, came home, watched TV, went to bed.

Even the *home* part of the equation seemed unsatisfactory of late. He was aware suddenly that his house didn't have any character. It had no warmth and no charm. It looked faintly sterile and unfriendly. It didn't *welcome* him when he got home from work. The mad-

dening part of it all was that his house—and his life—
had contented him perfectly just a short while ago.

He looked at the jacket he was having cleaned and
frowned. Was it the same jacket he'd worn at Harry's
wedding? Maybe that was bad luck, given how Harry's
marriage had ended.

Justin snorted at himself. He reminded himself who
he was. He was a man who dealt in practicalities, not
luck. Renegade thoughts about home-decor dissatis-
faction did not reflect who he was either! Still, he
studied the jacket hanging from the peg in his truck.
It was a nasty shade of blue with a faint herringbone
pattern in it. It would be a shame if it was that ugly
and unlucky.

The truth was, he wouldn't be caught dead in it if it
wasn't his only sports jacket. Shopping was out of the
question. There was no menswear store in Hunter's
Corner, plus shopping, especially for clothing, was only
for truly momentous events. Truly momentous events
were delegated stingily—weddings, funerals, christen-
ings—and the poetry reading did not begin qualify.

And he was a man who knew, since he'd kept himself awake most of last night debating the question of
whether he should try to get a new jacket.

Still, he didn't want to hurt anyone's feelings by
dressing wrong, so Justin hoped to hell Fred knew what
he was talking about.

It occurred to him, as he hopped out of his truck and
retrieved the jacket, that he had not been this nervous
about a date for a very long time.

Of course, he had not been on a date for a very
long time.

"It's not a date," he told himself. A date might qualify as a momentous occasion, especially in his life.

If the poetry reading needed a label, Justin thought the word *experiment* might do nicely. He conceded an experiment was not such a bad idea at this point in his life.

So when was the last time he had been nervous about a rendezvous with the female of the species?

He distinctly remembered sixth grade. It had taken him a week to ask Rhonda Staltwelder if she'd go to a movie with him. His palms had sweated and his tongue had cleaved to the roof of his mouth. He'd dialed her number and hung up the phone half a dozen times before he had managed to hold on to the receiver long enough to spit out his question.

He could still hear the shrillness of her laughter. Of course, Rhonda had been in ninth grade at the time, the front-runner for the Hunter's Corner Harvest Princess competition. His aspirations had been ridiculous.

But really, since that one rather memorable failure, he couldn't remember being nervous around females. Girls liked him. They even liked him if he treated them badly, which he was now somewhat ashamed to realize he had.

The truth was, he couldn't ever remember caring all that much about the kind of impression he made. He'd always been a take-me-or-leave-me kind of guy. So this experiment and actually *caring* what Bridget thought of him was a brand-new—and not altogether welcome—experience.

He entered the cleaner's and froze.

Bridget Daisy had her back to him, handing a black

dress across to the clerk, but he would know the color of that hair and the sweet slenderness of the line of her back anywhere. He stuck his foot in the door before it slid all the way shut. With just a little luck he could slide back out of there without even being noticed.

Of course, when it came to Bridget Daisy, he should have realized luck—or fate or whatever you wanted to call it—did not exactly side with him. Because he hesitated for a fraction of a second, making note of the straight lines and uninspiring gray of the dress she was wearing, the practical black shoes.

And he'd been wasting all this time wondering what to wear? Sheesh. Her dress looked as if it had been modeled after a stainless-steel refrigerator.

The half second wasted on that trivial observation lost him his chance. Because she turned at precisely the same moment he was caught somewhere between coming and going.

"Oh!" she said. "Justin."

"Uh, hi." The dress faded into nothing, eclipsed by the pure green of her eyes, by the radiance of her skin, by the tentativeness of her smile. Her hair, where it had fallen out of its bun to lie on her shoulder, looked like fire against that dull gray color.

"What are you doing here?" she asked.

He would have thought the sign over the door and the jacket in his hand made that fairly obvious, but suddenly he was embarrassed.

If he told her he was getting ready for the poetry reading, then she'd know he was trying, a trifle desperately, to manipulate her impressions of him. She'd know he was trying way too hard. Every male knew that trying way too hard was the kiss of death, so he said with studied casualness, "Oh, I'm dropping off this suit jacket for Fred."

"That's nice of you," she said, beaming, apparently approving of saints.

He smiled, letting her have her illusions. If she ever did get to know him, it wouldn't last. Because if he knew her a little better, he'd probably say out loud the word that blasted through his head when he realized he'd had one thing to wear to her stupid reading and now he'd just killed that option.

"What are you doing here?" he said brightly, Saint-Justin-who-never-said-bad-words.

She wrinkled her nose. "Work clothes," she said.

They stood looking at each other. She tucked one slender leg behind the other, and he noticed the dress showed off her knees. The shoes weren't too bad from this angle either. They made her feet look tiny and ador-able, the kind of feet a man captured between his hands and nibbled the instep of.

"Your fence is just about finished," he said so she would never begin to guess he was fantasizing about slipping those sturdy shoes off her dainty feet and kiss-ing her insoles until she was begging him to stop.

"I saw that when I got home yesterday. Thank you. It looks beautiful."

Of course, fences did not look beautiful any more than any other ordinary, everyday thing—like potatoes or black sturdy shoes—looked beautiful.

She seemed to realize that. She blushed. "I meant well built."

And then she blushed harder, and he preened just a

little bit. She was looking at him in a way that made him think she wasn't talking about that fence at all.

"Thanks," he said, even though he sensed complications building around him like storm clouds.

Sure enough, here they came.

"I thought I might see you," she said after a moment and then added hastily, "you know, building the fence."

He had thought she might, too. But he hadn't wanted to see her and he'd carefully arranged his schedule to avoid encounters. Encounters with her led to weakness in him—agreeing to go to the poetry reading a case in point.

She was the kind of woman who had a man agreeing to poetry readings and heading for the dry cleaner's before he'd contemplated completely what it all meant. She was the kind of woman who had a man evaluating his lack of decorating skills before he exactly knew what happened. She was the kind of woman who had a man offering to take her fishing even though it was evident she was totally unsuited to the sport.

He hadn't wanted to see her for one very simple reason.

She made him lose control of his well-ordered world.

Totally.

Even dressed in a horrible gray dress, with her hair falling down and her makeup long since faded, she threatened everything in him that was rational.

Because right there in the dry cleaner's he lost control, he totally forgot the repercussions of tangling with her, he totally forgot the reasons, all of them good ones, that he didn't want to be around her.

He heard his own voice say, "You want to go grab a bite to eat or something?"

What was he thinking? He was fresh off work. There was a hole in the knee of his jeans and his shirt had concrete dust on it. Days of avoiding her, to capitulate to her charms so thoroughly on a chance meeting!

The only place he was going to be able to eat looking like this was Tony's, a rough-and-tumble bar on the edge of town that served great burgers along with quite a bit of rowdiness. Not that he needed to worry. She wasn't going to say yes. She was a woman of intelligence and refinement. She wasn't going to say yes to going for a bite to eat with a working man in torn jeans.

"Yes."

He started to worry. Hell, his buddies hung out at Tony's, each and every one of them who had been laughing at Miss Bridget Daisy since she had circulated her SOW/COW.

"I could go home and change," he said.

"You look great." There was that blush again. "I just meant you don't have to bother. Not for me." Her smile was sweet and shy, accepting of him.

It was that acceptance that made him feel unglued. He should think of an excuse to get away from her. He should slap himself on the forehead and say, gosh darn he'd forgotten he had a meeting with a customer in a few minutes. But looking into her eyes, he was reminded she just wasn't the kind of woman you could lie to and then live with yourself.

"You want to ride with me?"

He could tell she did, but she shook her head. "I have my own car."

"Just follow me then," he said.

She beamed at him as if she was going to dinner at a five-star restaurant.

Seeing Tony's through the brand-new eyes of a man who had invited a woman there he wanted to impress, it seemed like a faintly shoddy place, dark and well used. It smelled of spilled beer and old smoke, even though Tony had banned smoking over a year ago.

Justin's own name was still cut into one of the tables from his first time there, the day he'd turned legal. There were peanut shells on the floors, and the juke-box blared country. The boys could be counted on to be talking way too loud by early in the evening.

By which time he'd have her out of there.

He didn't want her to walk in alone, so he waited for her in the parking lot and then held open the door for her. He was aware, as she walked in, of the sudden silence in the room.

He slid her a look. It was as if the queen had stopped for a visit among the peasants. She had her chin tilted and was clutching her purse in front of her. Every other woman in the place had on low-slung jeans and a belly-button-revealing top. She should have looked out of place, like a schoolteacher who found herself accidentally in a Hell's Angels hangout. But strangely Justin didn't think she did look out of place. Standing there in her plain gray dress, he thought she looked like a ray of light.

And in some ways, wasn't that what she had been since the moment he had met her? Unexpected light in a world that had gone gray?

Before he could contemplate that very scary thought, Harry Burnside materialized at his side.

"Hello," he said, beaming at Bridget and ignoring his best friend. "Who are you, besides this town's best kept secret?"

"Bridget Daisy, Harry Burnside," Justin said, aware of a funny little reluctance to introduce them.

Harry was a lady's man.

She extended her hand. Harry eyed it with surprise, then bent over it and kissed it. Justin felt a strange desire to punch him in the mouth.

"Harry," she said, and her eyes found Justin's. "The practical joker, right?"

He recalled, startled, hc had mentioned Harry once, briefly at their first meeting. It would do good for him to remember she was one smart lady. Nothing got by her.

Harry suddenly went very still. "Bridget Daisy. I know that name. SOW COW. No."

"Yup," Justin said dangerously. Harry had never been one to get anything less subtle than a kick in the shin, though. "Having a bite to eat with me, her contractor."

"SOW COW nothing, you dog." An elbow ground into his ribs.

Justin gave his friend a look that spoke volumes about how unsafe it would be for Harry to go any further down that route.

He wasn't really sure what he had been thinking when he had blurted out his invitation to Bridget to join him for dinner, but he had probably imagined an evening somewhat like the one they had shared at her house, minus the annoyance of thc cat. Easy conversation, unexpected laughter. Maybe that expectation had caused him to issue the impromptu invitation.

But if that had been his expectation, he was disappointed. His table was literally swarmed. Every contractor in town who had snubbed her now seemed intent on making amends. She was promised a free birdhouse, someone offered to paint her fence, business cards were stacking up on their table in case she needed any other renovations done.

"This place is charming," she said in a gap between swarmings.

"Charming," he agreed, sending a mean look at Duncan Miller, who was heading over. Duncan swerved; maybe the mean look had reminded him he had been prepared to gouge Bridget out of nine thousand dollars for her fence.

"And the food is so good."

She was barely aware of the undertones of masculine energy swirling around them. He was so aware of it, so on guard, feeling so protective of her, he had barely tasted his burger. She seemed to be quite flushed by all the attention, giggling in a way that made her seem like a prom queen rather than the demure little librarian that she was. Maybe it had something to do with the mug of beer in front of her. But when he looked at it, she had barely touched it. Her water glass was empty, though.

He signaled for the check. "Sorry," he said. "I have to run." *He had a full evening ahead, planning what to wear to the poetry reading the following night.*

"Well, if your friend wants to stay—" Harry had always had a gift for materializing at exactly the moment when his intended prey was most vulnerable.

Justin gave Harry a glare that could have stripped paint.

But he needn't have wasted his energy. Bridget hadn't seemed to even notice Harry's suave good looks. She gathered up her things hastily, something like panic sweeping her face.

"Good grief, " she said. "I have to go! My poor cat!"

Suddenly she looked guilty and flustered. "'Bye Justin. Mr. Burnside." She practically bolted for the door.

"The cat," Harry said knowingly. "There's always something to mar perfection, isn't there?"

Justin agreed completely, but he hated the way Harry said that with a faint sneer in his voice, as if Bridget was so eccentric she could be written off. Justin was burningly aware that for the second time that night he had to resist an urge to punch his best friend right in the nose.

"Conan, I'm so sorry," Bridget said. She came through the door, tossed down her purse and lifted her cat. "You must have been so worried!"

Conan resisted her embrace, putting his paws on her shoulders and pushing back from her. Did he seem a trifle miffed, not worried?

She laughed at herself. *Now* who was assigning very human motives to a cat?

"Look," she said, setting him down, "I'll make it up to you." She opened some of the soft cat food she had recently acquired. Silly to think he could read that it said diet in small letters on the label.

The cat looked after, she went into her bedroom and did an experimental twirl in front of her mirror. Okay, in her gray dress and sensible shoes, a sex goddess she wasn't. And yet a strange thing had happened sitting in that quaint little establishment with Justin.

Bridget Daisy had felt beautiful.

Not because of all those silly contractors fussing over her either.

Because Justin had asked her to go with him. Because of the way he had looked at her, as if he was barely tasting that scrumptious burger, as if he might have to leap up and protect her from something at any moment.

With him, aware she sat in the circle of his protection, she had felt some of her wariness of men drop away. She had actually enjoyed the attention rather than being flustered by it!

She shouldn't have gone with him. Especially now. He had seen the black dress at the cleaner's and she had told him it was work clothes, not wanting him to know how hard she had been thinking about what to wear. Now she was back at square one. She closed her bedroom door so Conan wouldn't come in and get orange hair all over her clothes. Out came everything in her wardrobe again. She surveyed it with a critical eye.

She heard a piteous mew at the door and relented. She opened the door and scooped Conan into her arms.

"Don't you ever worry," she told him, dancing around her room with a wonderful sense of bliss. "You will always be my best guy."

But it felt so giddily wonderful that that might not always be true.

The next night, dressed in a plain black skirt that the cleaner's had managed to hem up in record time and a white blouse that was surprisingly fashionable considering it came from the dusty little mercantile on Main Street, Bridget answered the door.

Justin stood there in a plain black turtleneck and camel-colored jeans.

She was not sure she had ever seen a man so gloriously good-looking. His eyes skimmed her outfit and rested on the hem of her skirt.

Too short, she thought but nonetheless felt a rather wicked sense of enjoyment at the frank male appreciation in his eyes.

He had his hands behind his back, and with a self-conscious flourish he showed what he had hidden there.

He had a rose for her! Not a red rose either. A lovely ivory, dusted with peach at the tips. The scent coming off it was heavenly. And then, looking faintly embarrassed, he handed her something else.

She looked at the tiny can and burst out laughing.

"Tuna Wonder Whiskers," she said. "Conan's favorite. Isn't it Conan?"

But the cat was hiding under the kitchen table and refused to be coaxed out even for Wonder Whiskers. Not that she was going to bend over too strenuously in this skirt!

"How's he liking the door?" Justin asked. "With the fence done, he must be going in and out at will."

"Well, um, it seems to take him a while to figure out new things."

"He's not using the door?" Justin bent over and looked under the table.

Was that dislike in his face? Surely not. He had brought the cat a present!

But if she couldn't determine what was in Justin's face, Conan's was not nearly so difficult to read. Her cat did not like her beau. And animals were said to be uncanny judges of character! But she was not letting that niggling thought ruin her evening. She opened the can of food and put it in Conan's dish.

As she and Justin watched, he meandered over and eyed the offering suspiciously. He took a dainty bite, stuck his nose in the air and walked away.

"I guess he doesn't like that kind," Justin said, unperturbed. "Shall we go?"

But now Bridget wondered if her cat was ill. Conan was not one to refuse food.

With one last worried look his way, she let Justin help her with her coat, and they went out the door.

"Oh," she said as they entered the library, "what a wonderful turnout. There must be a dozen or so people here."

All of whom seemed to be eyeing the length of her skirt and Justin with very avid interest. She introduced him to the members of the poetry club and watched with delight as he quickly became the center of attention. The club was ninety per cent female, and not a one under forty, but obviously age did not dim one's appreciation of a good man!

The members of the club looked distinctly annoyed when she called them to order, though they quickly got into the reading. Each person read one original poem and then shared a favorite. Tennyson, Blake, Frost and Dickinson shared the stage with very amateur but heartfelt offerings.

Bridget slid Justin a look as Myrtle Sopwit recited her original work with closed eyes and her hand over her heart.

"Tree, in my front yard," Myrtle cried with enthusiasm, "you art a most glorious bard, your green leaves sing songs so fine, oh, how lucky you art mine."

Was he going to laugh out loud? She wanted to herself but bit the inside of her cheek and hoped Myrtle was finished.

Myrtle, however, was gathering steam, her high-pitched voice ascending into a furious crescendo. "Worm! Worm! In that tree, you art the enemy, chomping and chomping, you filthy swine, you bring blackness to this heart of mine."

Bridget felt his shoulder shake treacherously where it was touching hers. She tried to think of other things as Myrtle launched into her final stanza. His hand found hers and closed around it, and suddenly and thankfully the adventures of Myrtle's tree faded. He played his thumb across the palm of Bridget's hand, and the sensation became Bridget's whole world.

Myrtle finished with a flourish, bowing deeply to her wonderful friends, who applauded her effort with enthusiasm.

Justin released Bridget's hand to applaud, but his eye caught hers, and she saw the smile in it, the glint of amusement.

The only male member of the poetry club gave his offering last. Leonard Wilthope stood shyly, shuffling from foot to foot. "The weather gathered darkly, like the hoof of a heifer…"

Thankfully Justin's hand found hers again, and his thumb did that wicked thing against her palm. All the while he looked straight ahead, for all the world a man entranced by how badly a simile could be slaughtered.

There was coffee and cake after the readings, and to her amazement, Justin did not hustle her out of the building as if the seat of his pants were on fire. Instead he mingled, and she realized he knew many of these people. She heard them mention his father to him again and again.

Finally, as the last ones left, she locked the library doors.

"The library looks wonderful," he told her. "Not the dusty old tomb I grew up with at all."

"Thank you," she said. "It always was a beautiful building, it just needed some tender, loving care."

"You strike me as someone good in the TLC department."

"I do?"

"For instance, you're very good to those old people," he told her. "It's obvious they adore you."

She was faintly disappointed. She had hoped he was going to link her great capacity for TLC to something more personal, like himself. But perhaps the front steps of the library was not the time.

She followed his lead and kept it slightly impersonal. "They seem to adore you, too," she said.

"Yeah, I guess they're beginning to forgive me for raiding their gardens, stealing their mailboxes and leaving tire prints on their front lawns."

"I heard them talking about your father. What happened to him?"

He was silent for a long moment. "He died last year, after a long, long struggle with a terrible illness."

Just like that, it was very personal. She sensed how hard it had been for him to say that, sensed that he felt vulnerable and sensed there was only one way to respond. From her heart. She touched his cheek tenderly. She looked into his eyes and saw in them a story of courage and sorrow. She saw his strength was not just physical but something much, much deeper.

"He had Alzheimer's," Justin said, his voice ragged. "Bridget, he went from being this big, strong, successful man to being an out-of-control child. At first it was little things. He couldn't remember a name, he forgot appointments. Then it was bigger things. The neighbors calling to report, always with such regret, that this man who had been their friend was peeing in their hedges and pulling up their carrots.

"My dad," he said, his voice choked, "who had always been so dignified and so respected... " His voice faded away.

"I'm so sorry, Justin."

"Finally it sucked the color from my world," he admitted. "Every day just felt like an exercise in survival. The joy was gone, the desire to meet new people or try new things. Everything seemed to take energy, and my Dad took every single bit I had for a long, long time."

"I hope the color comes back in your world," she said softly.

He touched her hair and gazed into her eyes in a way that made her heart beat way too fast.

"It is," he said softly. "The color is coming back in my world. And Bridget, I think it's because of you."

She didn't know what to say. She was not sure anyone had ever said anything quite so lovely to her.

She was not used to compliments and didn't know how to accept it graciously. "Oh, no," she protested. "I'm sure it's not—"

But she never finished. Because right there on the front steps of the library, under the street lamp, where anybody in Hunter's Corner could see them, he kissed her.

He kissed her so thoroughly that she didn't really care one whit who was watching. All she cared about was the sweetness of his lips, the drugging honey of his kiss, the warm shelter of the strong arms that gathered her close.

All she cared about was the color, brilliant and shining, that flooded her world, a world she had not even known was black-and-white.

Chapter Eight

Conan awoke from a troubled sleep to hear a commotion on the front steps of the house. *Burglars,* he thought and made it from the seat of the off-limits chair to under it in the blink of an eye. Normally he might try to protect the place, but he was certain he was still suffering PTSD.

More scuffling noises outside the door and then a faint, muffled giggle.

Giggle?

He eased out from under the chair, leaped silently onto the couch, nosed open the venetian blind just a crack.

His eyes widened, then closed to menacing slits. Bridget and Pest were on the front steps. Their heads were way too close together. It looked as if Pest was sniffing her neck, and she had her head thrown back as if she was enjoying it.

Conan didn't recall that she enjoyed *him* sniffing her neck.

Oh, he should have seen this coming from the moment Pest had appeared in uncharacteristically clean clothing, bearing some kind of corny flower for Miss Daisy.

How had he missed it? Oh, yes, he'd been thrown off guard when Pest had produced the can of Wonder Whiskers. He had actually debated the possibility it was a peace offering!

When it had turned out to be tuna-flavored, his guard should have snapped back into place! He should have immediately suspected that this man only wanted to eliminate the feline threat. After all, tuna had been his lure of choice last time, and look at the result! The lunch-bucket fiasco!

But oh, no, ever trusting and chronically feeling deprived because of the stupid diet, Conan had been unable to resist a tiny sample bite. To his great distress, Conan found the tuna very unsettling. At the time he had thought it was a residual symptom of post-traumatic stress.

Now, watching the performance on the front porch, he wasn't so sure. Pest was after *his* mistress. He was a primal sort of man.

No doubt the competition had to be eliminated.

Had the tuna been poisoned?

Miss Daisy tumbled through the door. Her hair was a mess and her face was on fire. Her clothing was faintly disheveled.

Miss Daisy in disheveled clothing? Miss Daisy's hair a mess? It was a sign that things were much worse than Conan could have imagined!

"Good night, Justin," she called softly and waggled her fingers at the man who was sauntering down her front walk as if he owned the earth.

She closed the door, leaned against it and sighed. It was a sigh like nothing Conan had ever heard before, as if she had hiked to the top of a mountain and been left breathless and awed by what she had glimpsed there.

Conan slid off the back of the couch and went over to her, rubbed her legs possessively and vigorously. His mission was twofold: to bring her back into this world and to mark his territory with his scent.

Miss Bridget Daisy belonged to him!

She shook herself from her trance, reached down and tickled his ears and chucked his chin.

"What a handsome fellow you are," she said, but her expression was faraway and dreamy, and he knew she was thinking of someone else.

He had seen firsthand that the human female could have a treacherous heart. But Miss Daisy? No! It wasn't possible. She was being charmed. It wasn't her fault that she was weak and susceptible. That man was diabolically crafty.

Because over the next few days even Conan found himself being charmed, albeit reluctantly.

The fence and cat door, which Conan was still boycotting, had apparently come with the world's best guarantee, because they seemed to be the excuse for Justin's frequent drop-ins. A new hinge for the cat door to see if it would swing better. Several shades of fence stain for her to choose from. A modification to the gate.

But come on! Always at supper time? Always as she was just getting home from work?

Conan could see through the flimsy excuses and he was pretty sure that Miss Daisy could, too but she just didn't seem to mind.

And damn, the man was proving hard to resist, even for one as determined as Conan. Because on every one of Justin's "fence maintenance" visits, he brought something for Conan. With a certain amount of self-disgust, Conan found himself starting to anticipate the visits.

His shield of dislike and suspicion was disintegrating under the onslaught of adorable—and largely edible—little gifts. Nothing was poisoned, as far as he could tell. Perhaps Pest had decided you could catch more cats—and cat owners—with kibble than with vinegar.

"Justin!" Bridget squealed at the latest offering. "This looks like a real mouse!"

Give, give, Conan panted at her feet.

"I know," Justin said, watching her intently, as if her squeals were irresistibly cute. "The label says it's made with real mouse fur."

"Gross," Bridget said, but she was laughing. She handed over the mouse.

Conan scurried under his favorite chair with it. Heaven! The fur was real, divinely scented. His new friend dispensed droplets of catnip with very little prodding! Conan hardly even noticed that Bridget and Justin left for a walk without him.

"He's on a diet," Bridget protested the next night when Justin appeared with a tin of Fancy Dinner.

"One little can of liver won't hurt him!"

Right on, Conan thought and threw his dignity to the

wind when the liver pâté hit his dish. He buried his face right in it. By the time he came up for air, it didn't matter one little bit to him that Bridget and Justin were out on the porch swing, rocking slowly and watching the stars come out.

Since his lunch-bucket incident, rocking made Conan sick anyway.

The following night, both he and Miss Bridget were waiting for the sound of that truck to pull up.

"What do you suppose he brought us tonight?" she mused as they both ran to the window and watched Justin get out of his truck.

Conan was hoping for a live gerbil in a wheel!

"Bicycles!" she exclaimed. "He's unloading bikes from the back of his truck."

Conan tried to hide his disappointment. Cats did not ride bikes! But he needn't have worried, because when Justin came up her steps two at a time, he had not forgotten Conan.

"Look what I found for him," he said, grinning at Miss Daisy. "Dr. Innard's Rodent Pies."

"That's sick!" Miss Daisy said, but you could tell she didn't really think so. "Conan, do you want a rodent pie?"

Do I?

She opened the pie and put it in his dish.

"Whoo! This can't be edible." She held her nose prettily.

There was no accounting for taste! Conan breathed deeply. The bouquet was unbelievable!

He glanced up as they headed out the door. Miss Daisy had changed into bike-riding apparel. He couldn't help but gawk. Was that his Miss Daisy in shorts that rode halfway up her thigh? Justin was gawking, too.

"Lady," Justin said, his voice a growl of pure appreciation, "those legs could get you into the leg hall of fame."

"There is no leg hall of fame," she said and hit him prettily on his arm.

He pretended to wince. "Well, there should be. I think I'll build one right there on Main Street, in the empty lot across from your library. You can be the first inductee. We'll have a ceremony and invite the poetry club. I'll ask Miss Sopwit to write a poem in honor of the event."

"Stop," she begged, laughing.

But apparently he was just warming up. In a voice that hurt Conan's ears but that Miss Daisy apparently found hilarious Justin said, "Leg, leg you're so fine, better than beery brine."

"Stop it! That's awful."

Truly awful, Conan agreed. So why was she encouraging him by laughing so hard, her normal dignity totally swept away by her unladylike guffaws? They went out the door with Justin still reciting full steam in that horrible falsetto, rhyming *legs* with *begs* and getting in something about kissing her kneecaps. Good grief! And she thought Dr. Innard was sick?

The truth was, Conan was glad when they were gone. Distractions were not wanted. Conan needed to give his full attention to the feast in his cat dish. He took a dainty bite. Delirium! It was so good he thought he might faint.

He wanted to savor, but he gulped, and all too quickly he was licking the last tidbits from the sides and bottom of his bowl. Feeling drunk with happiness, he dragged himself under his chair. Getting on top of it at this point was out of the question. He cleaned his paws and his face, deeply contented. Speaking of hall of fame deservees! Dr. Innard should be awarded the title of Honorary Cat. The pie was superb.

Yes, sharing Miss Daisy wasn't nearly as bad as Conan had first anticipated it might be. He had to put up with a lot of talk about Justin, when he had formerly had the spotlight to himself, but it was a suitable trade-off.

Because the best part was that Miss Daisy was so enthralled with her growing relationship that she seemed to be getting more and more lenient about her diet ideas. In no time Conan felt things would be back to normal. Better than normal if you counted Rodent Pie.

He tucked his slightly bedraggled mouse friend between his paws, curled up contentedly and went to sleep.

Much later, Miss Daisy came in. She was holding two crushed roses as if they had appeared out of midair, spun of magic and dreams. Conan, through his one grumpily opened eye, noted the glow of color in her normally pale cheeks. He noted the way her hair swung, free and glossy. He noticed how she moved with so much more confidence, with a new ease. Her eyes shone. She licked her lips, and he realized they looked slightly puffy.

She looked young and carefree, she was glowing with an energy that Conan had not known she possessed before the presence of a man in her life.

"He's going to come over and watch a movie tomorrow night," she confided in Conan. She reached under the chair and gave his belly a scratch. He tried not to burp. His belly still felt delightfully, uncomfortably full.

I vote for Willard. He tried good old telepathy to get his movie choice to her. She obviously wasn't receptive, because the next night when she put the movie in, it was *Fried Green Tomatoes*. She and Justin sat on the couch, not enough room between them for a cat.

At least, Conan thought, settling in on the back of the couch, the movie was about food. After a few minutes, though, it became very apparent to him the movie had nothing to do with food.

"This is one of my favorite movies of all time," Miss Daisy confided to Justin in one of the slow moments, of which Conan was finding there were many.

"Mine is *Road Warrior*."

"Please be kidding. Are you kidding?"

He laughed. "Yes."

"So what is it really?"

"Friday the Thirteenth."

For some reason she found that ridiculously funny and dissolved into giggles. Even if so much laughing chased away her normal dignity, Miss Daisy did look pretty when she laughed like that.

Apparently Justin thought so, too, because he made her laugh harder when he said, "No, wait. *Jerry Springer, Uncensored.*"

"Who is Jerry Springer?" she managed to ask when she stopped laughing.

Justin shook his head, kissed her lightly on the lips,

turned his attention back to the movie. The space between them on the couch had grown even smaller.

"No," she insisted. "You have to tell me. Your *real* favorite movie."

"A Beautiful Mind," he said finally, as if he was confessing to liking women's underwear. Which no doubt he did—hopefully on women, Conan thought.

"Oh," she breathed, and for some reason that had been just the right answer. She nestled in closer to him, and their hands intertwined.

And Conan thought, *Hey, a cat can be wrong. Maybe this is going to work out after all.* She was happy. He was happy. He thought about his new bag of treats that Justin had brought for him tonight—turkey crunchies with the hard outsides and the soft centers—and began to purr.

To his surprise, Justin reached up with his free hand, slid it under him and put him on his lap. He stiffened momentarily, but Justin found that sweet spot right underneath Conan's chin and scratched nice and hard, not those dainty little scratches Miss Daisy gave him. Before Conan knew quite what had happened, he fell fast asleep, right in the lap of the man who was supposed to be his enemy. Conan didn't wake up again until the show was over. He barely stirred when Justin slid him off his lap onto the couch. He noticed sleepily that Miss Daisy walked the Pest to the door and went outside with him. They were out there for an awfully long time.

And when she came in, she sat back on the couch and pulled Conan onto her lap.

"A Beautiful Mind is his favorite movie," she whispered. "He liked *Fried Green Tomatoes.* He *really*

liked it. Conan, he said he'd watch *Shakespeare in Love* with me."

She was babbling, he was trying to sleep.

"On our bike ride, he stopped and picked me roses from the town flower bed. He got thorns in his hands and then he had to carry the flowers in his front pocket, and they scraped him the whole way."

Big deal. Trying to catch a few winks here.

"He makes me laugh. My face hurts from laughing sometimes. I've never laughed so much in my whole life."

Okay, already.

"I feel alive, Conan. I feel as if I am truly one hundred per cent alive, engaged in the process of living, not just going through the motions."

Yada, yada, yada.

"I see things I've never seen before—like those little birds at the feeder look like they've been dipped in cranberry juice."

Well, if we're going to talk birds, I might rouse myself.

"Conan," she whispered, "I'm falling in love with him."

He jolted fully awake and stared at her.

Love? Oh, he remembered that word. It had prefaced the kiss of death in his former life.

And he had allowed all this to happen, sitting back enjoying his treats as if there wasn't going to be a price for them! He had allowed himself to be lulled—no, bribed—into a false sense of security.

Justin was off his list of tolerated people.

And as if to cement his fate, the next night Justin arrived with the most inappropriate gift!

"See," he said waving a rubbery lump in front of Conan's nose. "It squeaks." To enforce this statement Justin squeezed the object, and it replied with a series of wheezing squawks.

Conan backed away, his new wariness about Justin helping him to find the whole concept of the toy stupid and distasteful. Was he supposed to be excited by the fact that it emitted horrible noises?

Miss Daisy laughed. "Oh, I think that might be a dog toy. That's why Conan doesn't like it."

Conan balked at the rubber object. A *dog* toy? Oh, yes, the man's true colors were starting to show now.

The revolting toy was dropped on the floor.

"I signed us up for a mixed pool tournament to-night," Justin told Bridget.

"Do you mean billiards or swimming?"

Justin laughed. "Billiards. Don't call them that at Tony's, though. I'd be the laughingstock of the town."

Conan glared at Miss Daisy. Pick up on that, sweet-heart. He's worried about getting laughed at because of you.

She didn't pick up on it. "A mixed pool tournament? I don't know how to play pool, Justin!"

"It's just for fun." He leaned close to her. "I'll teach you how to play. We could clean up. You strike me as a fast learner."

"Not at sports!"

"Pool is not a sport. Wrestling is a sport. I could teach you how to do that, too."

He raised a wicked eyebrow.

"No, thanks, let's stick with pool."

She was blushing wildly and happily, as if somehow

the prospect of rolling around on the floor with him se-
cretly thrilled her. Conan wished he could throw up on
Justin's shoe again, but his digestive system seemed to
be working perfectly. You could never count on a hairball to be there when you truly needed it.

"If you're a quick learner, we could win a prize,"
Justin said. "They have some great prizes at these mixed
tournaments."

"Really? What?"

"Free movie rentals. I don't actually want to pay for
Shakespeare in Love."

"Oh," she said, "just when I was thinking you were
the man of my dreams."

Yeah, Conan thought, *he nearly had me fooled, too*.
He watched as, unaware of the danger she was in, Miss
Daisy allowed the Pest to help her with her jacket. Then
they were gone.

Conan moved in stealthily on the loathsome toy,
fully intending to kill it, a practice run for what he intended to do to the Pest.

His back arched, his eyes bulged and he let out a
short hiss when he saw what it was. Grotesquely de-
picted on the toy was a fat orange cat riding—or stuffed
into—a black inner tube. Big white letters spelled out
B-I-T-E M-E! Conan sounded them out carefully. Reading was not his forte.

"Bite Me!" he finally spat out.

The awful message was clear! This was an item clearly
designed for vicious, gross dogs to tear apart! Was Pest's
message conscious or unconscious? Either way, the end
result was the same: in some part of his heart he harbored
the desire to have a dog rip poor little Conan into shreds.

Conan's bowels suddenly felt weak and he high-tailed it down the stairs to his basement litter box. He skittered to a halt. Shock coursed though his body. There was a sand-coated lump in it!

Never mind Shakespeare in love! This was Miss Daisy in love?

Miss Daisy in her proper frame of mind never allowed disgusting buildup. In fact, for as long as he could remember, the box was cleaned instantly.

Conan contemplated the box. He was in more danger than he had realized. Pest was out to get him, but Miss Daisy might finish him off with neglect!

This was probably only the beginning. One lump would become two, then…oh, he couldn't bear thinking about it! But he did anyway. His mind wandered from nasty litter boxes to food dishes left empty or unwashed, water dishes growing stale, bedding not cleaned.

He was too depressed to make the stairs. He found a pile of rags behind the furnace and lay down. A long, long time later, he heard the front door open and crept up the stairs. He sat on the top one, where he could hear them.

"See, I told you you'd be good at it," Justin told her.

"I won a prize for being the worst pool player in the history of the tournament."

"I think you clinched the title on that shot where you flubbed the ball and it hit the lady at the next table in the forehead."

"Didn't I embarrass you?"

"Hey! A week of free beer is nothing to scoff at."

Silence.

Conan peered around the basement door. Just as he had suspected! The silence was caused by that joining of lips and sucking that he found nearly as offensive as his uncleaned litter box.

I'll show them. He used his loudest walk to march toward them.

They didn't even look up or unlock lips.

Claws bared, he prepared to do what needed to be done. Conan, prepare to launch!

Before he could make his move, Conan was stopped dead in his tracks by Justin's words.

"Bridget, what would you think about going away with me for the weekend? I promised you a fishing trip, and a friend of mine has a cabin."

Conan sat down with a shocked plop. A weekend with a man? *Miss Daisy, don't do it!*

To her credit, she was hesitating.

"It will all be on the up and up, Bridget. The cabin has two bedrooms."

"Oh! Of course, then!" Her hesitation melted. Smiling from ear to ear, she declared, "Oh, I would simply love that, Justin."

Two bedrooms, my foot, Conan thought. Didn't she watch Discovery Channel at all? Didn't she pay attention? If you put two mammals of the opposite sex together in close quarters like that—oh, it didn't bear thinking about.

Pest knew! He knew the possibilities! He knew what could happen! Conan saw his knowing in his sly little grin as he touched her hair, trailed his thumb across her lips.

Conan raced up and bunted his legs, inserted himself between them. Meowed loudly and protectively.

Her smile fell. "Oh," she said. "I forgot."

Thank you. Forgotten kitty: litter box Exhibit A.

"Forgot what?" the Pest growled right in her ear.

"Conan," she said with effort. "What would I do with Conan?"

Conan couldn't help but preen at his importance.

Justin laughed. "I'm sure he's capable of taking care of himself for a couple days. Just leave out a five-gallon pail with some grub in it."

The insult of it! A five-gallon pail, as if he was a complete pig. He probably didn't eat five gallons of food in a year, if she did the math. But she was apparently in no condition to do math. Or to protest this affront to his character. Or to remember her duties as a cat owner.

"I guess people do that all the time, don't they? Leave their cats alone?"

"All the time," Justin said without one iota of feeling, unless that feeling was glee.

Yup, here it came. The strategic phasing out of the feline. Conan gagged as if he had the world's biggest hairball. Bridget had not even registered a token protest at the idea of letting him feed out of a slop bucket for days like some disgusting farm animal.

This trip is pure and simply not going to happen, Conan vowed icily. *Nothing will stop me from ruining it.*

He gagged a few more times, but neither of them noticed. He flopped dejectedly on the floor and glared at them with his famous if-I-was-bigger-I'd-kill-you look.

"Do we need to bring food?" Bridget asked, the thrill of having accepted the invitation making her voice rather breathless. "Would you let me look after the food?"

Oh, sure, worried about food for *them* now that slopping the cat was no longer an issue.

"No," Justin said hastily.

Hello! He doesn't like your cooking! He only wants one thing. But Miss Daisy was not on the receiving end of well-meant messages from her cat.

"I'll look after the food," Justin said, his voice all that soft charm that Conan had once almost fallen for himself. "I'll look after everything, Bridget. All you have to do is be waiting at the door at nine o'clock on Saturday morning."

He'd look after everything, all right, Conan thought cynically. He had no time to lie about feeling sorry for himself.

He had so little time and so much to do.

Bridget twirled in front of the mirror at the little boutique. Crazy to take an afternoon off of work to go shopping, but the truth was, she had nothing suitable to wear for a weekend at a cabin. And she was leaving tomorrow morning!

Not that she was at all sure this dress was suitable. The sundress was buttercup-yellow, clingy and flirty and like nothing the old Bridget Daisy had ever worn before.

The dress transformed her from an old-maid librarian into a sexy siren of a woman. Well, maybe that was going too far, but it certainly was sexy, with its high hem and low neckline. Could she? Should she?

"Bridget," she said to herself, "why are you so afraid to make a mistake?"

Actually she knew exactly why she was so afraid to make a mistake. Because her mother had made one, and a five-year-old child had paid for it in the currency of broken hearts.

It was time to leave that behind her. To trust, to take chances, to live!

The new her, the woman that Justin West looked at with such awe and tenderness and hunger, was taking the dress. Period. She could decide later if she actually had the nerve to wear it.

Along with the dress, she was taking the red bathing suit that her mother would have said clashed with her hair, the hooded black jogging suit with the flattering jacket and the low-slung pants and the jeans that looked as if they had already been washed four hundred times and fit her as though they were painted on. She had picked out three pairs of shorts that were a teeny bit too short and one pure white tank top that showed her belly button.

"Bridget," she told herself, "keep this up, and next thing you know, you'll be getting your belly button pierced."

So the thought of belly-button piercing intrigued her just a tiny bit. It was as if she had been living in a prison, the walls made of her own dos and don'ts and reinforced with her doubts and inhibitions.

Justin was breaking her out.

"No belly-button piercing!" she told herself firmly. She was already way over budget!

She glanced at her watch and gave a little squeal. While she was in the big city, she did need to get her hair cut and had signed up for one session at the tanning booth. Hopefully it would be enough so that she wouldn't do her normal burn-red-as-a-lobster-and-have-to-stay-in-the-rest-of-the-weekend thing.

Though having to stay inside a little cabin all weekend with Justin….

She sighed, paid for her purchases, trying very hard not to notice she had spent approximately two weeks' wages, and moved on.

By the time she drove home it was nearly nine o'clock at night. She had known she would be late, so she had done a dry run on Justin's suggestion she leave the cat alone. She had left the cat door unlocked, though to her knowledge he had not once used it.

She had left some dry cat kibble in a bowl for him, put out ample fresh water, made sure his litter box was clean. Still, as she put her key in the door, she was aware she felt guilty, as if she had been neglecting her cat shamefully. The truth was, she felt a little guilty about leaving him on his own this weekend. She had stopped and bought him a few of those little sushi rolls he liked to assuage her own conscience.

"Conan," she called, coming in the door. "I'm home."

No answer. She checked the kibble dish and found it untouched.

After searching room to room, she had the terrifying thought he might have gone outside and gotten away. There was no way he could get over the fence, but maybe the gate had been left open. But a careful inspection of the yard showed the gate was secure and Conan was nowhere to be seen. She searched her house again, somewhat frantically. She thought she heard a small, weak sound.

Bridget hurried down the basement stairs. Finally, following the sound of one more piteous weak cry, she found him. Conan was lying on a pile of rags behind the furnace. He didn't even lift his head, just blinked once very slowly.

She lifted him quickly and brought him upstairs. His heavy body was limp in her arms.

What was wrong with him? "Did you hit your head again?" she asked him, cradling him to her. "Or did you go out in the yard and eat something you shouldn't have?"

It had never occurred to her before how easy it would be for a cat hater to throw poison over her fence.

"Bridget," she told herself, "take a deep breath. You are totally overreacting. You're just sleepy, aren't you, Conan? I know what will wake you up! Some little sushi rolls. The ones with the shrimp in them."

She rifled through her bags, emerged triumphant with the sushi rolls. She put one in Conan's dish. He didn't move from where she had set him on the floor. She picked him up and brought him over, set him back down. His legs collapsed from underneath him like a card table folding. He strained his prone form toward the food dish, then sighed and gave up. Bridget took the sushi roll from his dish and held it in front of his lips. He licked it once weakly, then closed his eyes and sighed.

Now she knew she had an emergency on her hands. Trembling, she reached for her phone.

"Dr. Thornfield? It's Bridget Daisy. I'm sorry to trouble you at home. Conan is very ill. It's an emergency. You'll meet me at your office in five minutes? Thank you. Thank you so much."

Even though the evening was warm, she bundled Conan up in his sweater and headed for the vet's office.

Conan, as soon as he hit the car, did a complete turnaround. He tried to tear off his sweater and bounced from the front seat to the back. Thankfully the vet's office was only a few minutes away, or he might have caused an accident.

The vet met her and did a complete checkup on the now purring cat.

"But he was so sick," she said, feeling terribly foolish. "He wouldn't even lift his head to eat. I was sure he'd been poisoned."

The vet gave her an odd look, turned his back on her and opened a tin of food. The cat launched himself on it.

Bridget saw that look in the vet's eyes, remembered his last advice to her. He had told her she needed something more than her cat to care about.

"I have a boyfriend, you know!" she said defensively. "I have a whole life beyond my cat!" She had to bite her lip to keep from telling him about the yellow sundress.

"That's nice, my dear," he said cautiously, as if he had been confronted by a crazy woman.

She gathered up her cat, making a mental note to herself to find a new vet before she had any further emergencies that needed to be dealt with.

At home, the cat flopped bonelessly back on her kitchen floor. He ignored the sushi rolls and looked at her with helpless torment in his eyes. She tried everything. She even ordered pizza. No reaction from Conan, just those enormous eyes silently following her every move.

She hardly slept a wink into the wee hours of the night, though she had Conan right in bed beside her and she could feel the steady rise and fall of his tummy. In the morning she slept in. The ringing of the doorbell got her out of bed. Through the door window, Justin looked like a poster boy for Cabela's, World's Foremost Outfitter, standing on her porch in a floppy canvas hat and a fishing vest. The hat had fish hooks in it! His grin was easy and affectionate, and for a moment she could imagine his strong arms around her as he guided her cast with the fishing rod…. But then she remembered the sad truth.

She was not going anywhere. She stumbled over her unpacked shopping bags and flung open the door.

"Oh, Justin," she wailed, "I'm not going to be able to go!"

Chapter Nine

Justin looked at the woman who had just pulled open the front door of her house and felt his breath catch in his throat.

Nothing in his existence had prepared him for Bridget in pj's. She was adorably cute. The pajamas were a matching pair of hot-pink shorts with a tank-style top. The top had the astonishing message that Bookworms are Better. Her hair was in a delicious tangle, and the imprint of her pillow was pressed into one cheek.

In direct contrast to the cuteness, she was astonishingly sexy. There were those legs again, slender and well-shaped, and lots of them showing. Her toenails were painted a shade of pink that matched the pj's and was downright wicked. The cool morning breeze coming through the door was doing things to her chest that made him feel evil and perverted in contrast to her obvious innocence.

He hastily stepped in the door and shut it behind him.

"Better than what?" he teased her, as curious now about bookworms as he had ever been.

She looked at him blankly, and he registered the distress in her face. And then slowly her message sank in. *She wasn't coming?*

"You aren't going to be able to come to the cabin? Why? What's wrong?"

Without warning, she flung herself against his chest and pressed the full length of those delectable curves into him.

He felt suddenly dizzy with worry for her, her curves and the message on her T-shirt were wiped from his brain. He put her away from him gently, though he did not let go of her shoulders.

"What's happened?" he asked quietly. "Are you sick? Has something happened to someone in your family?"

She took a deep, shuddering breath. "Conan is sick."

He felt a little ripple of shock. He had expected her backing out of their weekend commitment would require a momentous excuse. Earthquake hits hometown. Cancer diagnosis. Fire destroys library.

But sick cat?

"Are you kidding?" he asked.

She missed the note of disbelief in his voice. "He's really, really sick. I can't even get him to eat."

He strove for patience. "Do you want to take him to the vet?" Good thinking, he congratulated himself. The vet would have a kennel. He could keep the cat under observation while Justin whisked Bridget away for a quiet weekend of firelight and fishing and whatever developed in between.

"I took him to the vet last night. He said he's fine. He did all kinds of tests." Her voice quivered. "He told me he might have feline leukemia."

The trauma of being told her cat might have leukemia rippled through her soulful eyes. "But he doesn't."

Justin was a little surprised by the depth of his own relief.

"The vet took his temperature and his blood pressure and did a very thorough checkup. Conan even ate something there. The vet said he's fine."

Well, we have it from an expert, then. Let's go.

"But I can just tell something is wrong with him. And I don't completely trust the vet. He's implied I might be a little too, um, focused on my cat."

Go figure.

The cat picked that moment to appear from down the hallway. He stopped lazily at his dish, stretched healthily, sniffed the contents and nibbled delicately on what appeared to be the sushi roll.

"He looks fine to me," Justin hazarded his opinion.

"I can't leave him when he's feeling like this."

Suddenly he got it. It wasn't about the cat at all, even if she might have convinced herself it was.

Justin looked at her long and steadily. "Maybe you just don't want to go."

"That's not it," she protested heatedly.

But suddenly, looking at how unconsciously sexy she was in those pajamas, he saw that he himself had had a narrow miss. Things would have heated up at that cabin whether he wanted them to or not.

Had he wanted them to? He was pretty sure he had.

He was a man. He had that evil tendency to be conniving without even knowing it.

And heating things up with Bridget Daisy would be a mistake of the irreparable variety. She wasn't that kind of girl. She was a forever kind of girl. The kind he liked the very least.

She had babies and picket fences written all over her. That's what the damned cat was about. She was rehearsing!

He glanced at the giant cat eating its sushi. Good grief! Conan was even about the same size as a baby. A good-sized baby, but a baby nonetheless.

Justin backed out the door as if his nose had been burned by a blowtorch. "Okay," he said hastily. "Call me when the cat gets better."

But he could hear the insincerity in his voice. He saw the hurt in her face, but he backed away from it and was out the door, down the steps.

"Wait," she called.

He turned back to her reluctantly.

"We could bring him with us."

For a full five or six seconds he didn't have a clue who she was talking about. When he realized she was suggesting taking her cat on *their* romantic weekend, Justin realized he had to make the break cruel and clean.

"Maybe the doc was right," he said. "You are too focused on your cat."

Ah, that was better, the anger flaring in her eyes instead of the vulnerability. Her voice was ice-cold considering the heat in her gaze. "I'm amazed that a big, strong guy like you would be threatened by one small cat."

"Yeah, that just goes to show you've led a very sheltered existence. For one thing, that cat is not small. And for another, you obviously don't know the first damn thing about big, strong guys. Probably not a whole lot about small, weak ones either."

She flinched visibly from that but said regally, "I should have stuck with my first instinct. Barbarian."

"I should have stuck with mine. T-R-O-U-B-L-E."

"Get off my property."

"Gee, I think I've heard that before, once or twice too often. I'm getting off, and gladly!"

"Good riddance."

"No more poetry readings for me, thank God."

"No more dingy pool rooms for me!"

"Good!"

"Good!"

He marched to his truck, hopped in and slammed the door before he was tempted to get the last word. You never would get the last word with a woman like her. Words were her specialty, for Pete's sake. She was the town guardian of them. She had millions and millions of them at her disposal. He, on the other hand, was a heathen, completely unsuitable in every way.

All the way home he thanked his lucky stars for that fact, for the fact he had been brought to his senses. A weekend with Bridget Daisy. What had he been thinking?

It was craziness. It was craziness from the first moment he had lain eyes on her. Thankfully he had been thrown a thread of sanity by fate and he had grabbed onto it.

And he remembered uneasily his feeling of distress when he'd seen her face and known something was wrong.

It was a replay of the last five years, when something had always been wrong.

He didn't want to feel fear anymore. Or helplessness. He reminded himself that he really didn't want to feel anything at all.

Not for her. And not for her cat either. Oh, yeah, his stomach had knotted up like a Boy Scout's practice rope when she had said Conan might have leukemia.

Here was a truth his father had taught him: caring hurt. It reached places inside a man that he was content to not know existed and filled those places with pain so deep and abiding it felt as if it would never heal.

If ever there was a man who was an expert on shutting down those pesky feelings, it was Justin West.

He didn't have a five-hundred-channel satellite server for nothing. He closed all his drapes against the promise of a sunny day, made himself a big bowl of popcorn and cracked a beer. Only ten in the morning? So what? That's what being a bachelor was all about. It was about not having to answer to anyone and not having to care about anything except the baseball schedule. In a pinch he could watch golf or old *Cops* reruns.

If the phone rang, he was going to ignore it. It would only be her anyway.

Was he disappointed when the phone didn't ring? Maybe. Did he wonder, in unguarded moments, how the cat was doing? Maybe. Did he try and figure out whether she had really hated the pool hall and why she'd been so good at pretending she hadn't if she had? Maybe. Did he contemplate the hurt he'd seen in her eyes and wonder if there was something he should be doing about it? Definitely. But he resisted all impulses.

He spent the weekend caved up, and on Monday he was thankful for houses to build and deadlines to meet. He was thankful for how a man could drive himself physically to the point where his mind didn't even work anymore. And when his cell phone rang, interrupting his work, he was aware he felt impatient even before he knew who it was. But his impatience died when he heard Fred's voice.

"Bridget didn't come to work today," he said, and Justin could not miss the note of accusation in his voice. "She told the volunteer library assistant she was sick."

There was that pesky pang of pure worry again.

"I'm sorry to hear that," Justin said flatly.

"You don't know nuthin' about it?"

"No."

"She's never called in sick before."

"Fred! Everyone gets a cold now and then." But his mind was doing terrible things. The cat had been sick. She had caught some dread disease from it. They were both lying over there, failing fast, weak, *needing* him.

Too bad he was the man who had vowed never to be needed again.

"If you done something to hurt her, I'm gonna have to whup ya."

In any other circumstances, that might have actually been funny—a bent-over old man who weighed about a hundred and ten pounds threatening to whup him. But somehow it wasn't funny at all.

"I didn't do anything to her," Justin said. "We had plans this weekend. She canceled because her cat was sick."

He didn't elaborate on what those plans had been.

He hadn't told Fred he was taking Bridget away for the weekend. Fred would not have approved of that. Fred was an old-fashioned kind of guy.

And Bridget was an old-fashioned kind of girl.

Thank God it hadn't worked out. Old-fashioned girls wanted things. Frightening things. Like rings and church bells.

And don't forget babies.

A renegade thought—of what kind of baby he could make with Bridget—pierced his heart. On the other hand, he bet a man worried about a baby, especially if it was his baby, nonstop. Every cry, every spit-up, every fall. No, thanks.

Justin was suddenly and sadly aware of feeling as lonely as he had ever felt in his life. Which served him right for stopping work to answer the phone.

"Fred," he said without preamble, "don't get any ideas about me and Bridget Daisy. She isn't my type. And even if she was, my dad taught me a pretty hard lesson about loving."

"What was that?" Fred asked, and Justin thought he heard a distinct lack of sympathy in that cracked old voice.

He had to remind Fred, who'd been there every step of the way? "He taught me loving hurts like hell."

There was a long silence.

"You damn ignorant fool," Fred said, his voice snapping with anger. "That isn't what your daddy taught you about love."

And then Justin found himself holding the dead end of a phone.

He wanted to phone Fred back and demand to know

what he'd meant by that. But instead he threw down his hammer, hopped in his truck and went home to the welcome of his dark cave. He turned the TV back on. But now it didn't seem to matter what was on. Because he was thinking about his father.

And he knew Fred was absolutely right. His father would have hated that—that Justin thought his legacy to his son was a world of hurt.

It wasn't.

His father's love, before his illness, had been about unfailing generosity to those who had less than himself, unflinching loyalty to his friends, unfaltering love to his family.

His father's love had been about teaching a little boy to fish and driving him to hockey games and practices at unholy hours of the morning. His father's love had been by turns gentle and stern. His father's love had been like a beacon of light that guided him through those teenage years of hard drinking and fast driving. His father's love had believed the best of him when there was little evidence that it existed and had required more of him when Justin himself thought he had already given enough.

And after the onslaught of that horrible dignity-robbing illness, hadn't Justin learned still more about love from his father? Hadn't he learned that when a man thought he couldn't go on, couldn't do one more day, love gave him the strength to get back up to the plate? Hadn't he learned how love forgave and hoped and re-membered all that was best? Hadn't he seen how love made a man stronger and wiser and better than he had been before, even if he didn't want to be any of those things?

Was there the slightest possibility that all that suffering with his father, all the sacrifice, had made him a man he had not been before? A man with some depth, with a bit of compassion, with a touch of sensitivity?

A man worthy of a woman like Bridget Daisy?

Suddenly Justin West understood with absolute clarity why he had not even tried to talk Bridget into going to the cabin.

Because somewhere along the way, he had come to love her.

And love asked more of him than a weekend away with her.

He realized he could not love her and treat her without complete honor. He could not love her and not voice a commitment to her.

He could not love her for only a weekend.

He tried to tell himself she was crazy and eccentric and he was better off without her and her cat. But he knew he was never going to believe it, no matter how many ball games he found on TV or how much beer he drank. He was not going to believe it, even if he worked away every hour of every day for the next fifty or sixty years.

He looked at his clock. Much too late to call her and ask about Conan. Much too late to call her and make a declaration of love.

Maybe he needed to sleep on that anyway.

He did, and in the morning when he awoke, it felt clearer than anything had ever felt in his life.

He knew exactly what his father had taught him about love. it was worth it. That the price it extracted might be high, but it was worth it. That a life without

it was dull and gray and empty, just the way his had
been for far too long.

Bridget looked at herself in the mirror with distaste.
Her eyes were puffy and her nose was red. She looked
so awful, she had missed work today! She never missed
work. Now she'd played hooky on Friday, to go shopping, and was absent again today.

"If this is love," she said to Conan, "who needs it?"

She was not the kind of girl who ever rode roller
coasters. She didn't like that bottom-falling-out-of-her-
belly feeling. She didn't like thrills or excitement.

She liked quiet evenings with good books and her
cat. She had made her world as predictable as she could.
What she craved, ever since that terrible day twenty-one
years before when her father had walked out the door
and never looked back, was certainty.

"Certainty," she muttered. "As if Justin could have
ever given me that! Thank God I have you." She picked
Conan up, rocked him like a baby in her arms. Thankfully her companion, her friend, her soul mate, seemed
to have made a complete recovery from his mysterious
illness.

He licked a little ice cream smudge from the corner
of her mouth.

She had known from the moment she had first lain
eyes on Justin West that he was going to be a roller-
coaster kind of man. She had known that! What had
made her throw her normal caution to the wind?

Maybe hope in the beauty and power of love had survived somewhere in her damaged soul.

"Insanity," she told the cat. "Do you suppose he really hated the poetry reading? Of course he did! Who wouldn't? What kind of idiot invites a man like that to a poetry reading where Myrtle Sopwit is scheduled to recite? I'll tell you what kind. One like me!"

After one more loving squeeze, she set her cat down and wandered away from the mirror and back to her fridge. She pulled the Häagen-Dazs from the freezer. She was almost out of ice cream! She did not want to go to the store! Not looking like this.

"Can you phone-order Häagen-Dazs?" she asked out loud. The cat purred and rubbed himself against her legs.

She reached for the bag of cat treats, remembered Justin had given them to him and burst into tears.

"This is not who I am!" she told the cat. "I am not a weak sniveler! I am a strong, confidant woman! I have a challenging career! I have a university degree! I own my own home."

Funny how none of those things she had accomplished seemed to define success in the way they once had. Funny how her whole definition had shifted. Was it not a type of success to be able to let go? To laugh until your face hurt? To show people who you really were? Wouldn't the greatest success of all be to love even though love had devastated you? To get back up, brush yourself off, try again?

"Oh, pooh to all that philosophical horse patoot," she said and fed Conan the whole package of treats just so she could throw the wrapper in the garbage.

She decided she was getting rid of every single thing Justin had ever given her. She was cleaning him out of her house and her mind.

Even if she was brave enough—and ready enough—to risk loving him, she knew he was never calling again. She knew it. She had seen the look on his face when he'd left. She had heard the cruel sting of his words. Her face burned when she remembered. As if she was some crazy old maid who had put her cat ahead of him.

Well, that's exactly what she had done.

"And it was a good choice, too," she told Conan. Wasn't it? It was obvious to her now that whatever illness had overcome the cat had been temporary. He was perfectly healthy. She could have gone and spent the weekend with Justin. She had thrown away her chance for nothing.

But a chance at what?

She wasn't the kind of person who went for clandestine weekends with a man. Or any kind of weekend with a man.

She had an innate sense of what was right and what was wrong, and it deeply disturbed her how quickly she had been willing to compromise that for Justin's easy good looks and mesmerizing charm.

"I would have hated myself after," she told herself.

After what? He had said they would have separate rooms. But hadn't she known in some secret place inside of herself that the way things were going between them, they might have ended up in the same room?

"Fate intervened," she told herself firmly. Still, she took the remaining ice cream to bed. After a moment, she got up and found the phone book. She called the Hunter's Corner Food Barn.

"I'm afraid I'm a bit under the weather," she said in her very best under-the-weather voice. "Do you ever deliver to shut-ins? You do?" She sighed with relief and hung up the phone.

She might never have to go outside again.

A rebel part of her thought that maybe giving in to the occasional temptation of a clandestine weekend would be slightly preferable to life as an ice-cream-eating, bedridden hermit.

"My thinking is totally muddled," she confided in the cat, who was now on the bed with her, easing closer and closer to the discarded lid of the ice cream. "That's what love does, Conan. They should put a warning label on every single poem and book that sings its praises."

She fell asleep with one arm around the ice cream bucket and the other around her beloved Conan. Twice in the night her own tears running down her cheeks woke her up. But in the morning when she awoke, she was determined to be strong, to put the whole sorry incident behind her, to write it off as the most unfortunate lapse in judgement.

She would not give Justin the satisfaction of ruining her life. She was not going to lie there one more moment feeling sorry for herself. She was getting on with her life as if he had been no more than a little green blip on a radar screen.

No amount of makeup could repair her face. She would just say she had a terrible cold, accompanied by an eye infection. And then, braced to face the world looking like an old maid whose very dream had been destroyed, she went to the back door.

The cat door, never used, flapped in the wind. She realized with a start she had not seen Conan this morning as she'd gotten ready to resume her life.

Despite Justin's warnings, she had forgotten to latch the door. Was it flapping because something disgusting had come in or because Conan had gone out?

It soon became evident to her that the one thing she had left was gone. Conan was gone.

Conan knew his falsified illness had been a staggering success. For a while he savored the pure power of it. He alone, one kitty, had managed to stop the catastrophic weekend fishing trip from taking place. He had managed to get rid of Pest once and for all.

Even his fears that a severed relationship would mean returning to his grueling diet proved delightfully unfounded. Miss Daisy spent her time stuffing him with food and massaging him. But he was beginning to worry about all that salt water on his fur!

On the first night after the "incident" he hadn't worried one little bit about her silly uncalled-for emotions. She was young and strong. She'd get over it. Sooner or later she'd even realize that he, Conan, had done her a huge favor by ridding her of that predatory man. In the meantime, he was in the limelight, lapping up Häagen-Dazs and whole bags of treats.

By the second night, he was having doubts. Conan cuddled next to Miss Daisy and was disturbed by how restless her sleep was and by the tears that flowed from her broken dreams.

A yucky and foreign feeling pierced the self-centered panorama of his thoughts. Guilt. It was a guilt so deep and abiding he doubted that it could be drowned out with any amount of liver pâté and ice cream dots.

An astonishing realization came to him.

He had broken the ultimate cat code. Conan had fallen in love with Miss Daisy. And love changed everything. It made it unbearable to watch her cry herself to sleep. It made her pain his pain. It made him realize he would go to the ends of the earth for her, that he had done a terrible and selfish thing when he had chased Justin away rather than letting the human heart follow its natural course.

He sat up and stared at her sleeping, tear-streaked face. It was evident to him that he must now try to return to her what he had so selfishly taken away.

Conan knew what he had to do. He had to find Justin before Miss Daisy withered away into a helpless, hopeless wreck. It wasn't about who would feed him then! It really wasn't. For once, it was all about her.

He had liked it when she laughed. He had liked the glow in her eyes. Okay, the litter box had been unacceptable, but wasn't the happiness that had been in the house worth a few small sacrifices?

Conan padded out of the room and pushed through the cat door into the cool, crisp night air. Within the safety of the fence, he mulled over his plan.

If he could find Justin, Justin would return him to Bridget, just like before. Bringing the cat home would give Justin just the excuse he'd been looking for to come back here and save his pride at the same time. Besides, all you had to do was get those two together. The chemistry happened all by itself.

But how to find Justin?

A simple matter, really. Conan knew that because of his devotion to the Discovery Channel. Once he had watched a program about a family that had moved across the country and mistakenly left their cat behind. However, over a year later their old cat had remarkably reappeared at their new house, even though it had never been there!

Conan decided that if that cat could trust his instinct, walk across the entire country and locate a place that it had never been, then he could easily navigate across Hunter's Corner to a location where he had been, even if at the time he'd been incarcerated in a lunch bucket.

In fact, the mission would probably take only a few hours. He could be back with the Pest before Miss Daisy woke in the morning.

He scaled the fence with ease despite his slightly portly condition. He paused at the top and looked over at Miss Daisy's darkened bedroom window. He would have liked her to see that the fence was really no challenge to him and thought of yowling her awake. But then he reminded himself this mission was about her and reluctantly gave up the opportunity to show off the athleticism she was so inclined to underestimate.

Everything will be okay again soon, Miss Daisy, Conan vowed. He leaped off the fence, paused and tuned into his intuition. *That way,* he decided even though his intuition reception seemed a little fuzzy.

Several hours later, in the gray predawn, Conan, gasping from exertion, surveyed his surroundings. Nothing looked even faintly familiar.

Uh, you were trapped inside a bucket, genius, he reminded himself. *Nothing is going to look familiar.* He dialed into the intuition and felt a moment's panic when he got a busy signal.

Doubt set in. He began to wonder if maybe, just

maybe, his perfect feline radar had been temporarily thrown off while he was being bounced about in that lunch box. Could he just be following useless, scrambled coordinates?

Of course not.

Conan glanced about nervously. He thought he could smell raw unkempt-dog odors wafting from an alley to his right. How many stray, hungry dogs were there in Hunter's Corner anyway?

His mind flashed back to that horrible toy with the fat orange cat in the inner tube. Miss Daisy had thankfully thrown that away with the other things Justin had given her, but how many *dogs* in this town owned those toys and thought cat attacks were fun because of the unethical trade in cat-hating merchandise?

When he got out of this, he was going to become an advocate for cats everywhere. Good grief! Was he bargaining with the Great Cat Spirit?

He shuddered. Maybe this hadn't been such a good idea after all. Maybe he had been just plain stupid. He was all that Miss Daisy had now that Justin was gone. What if something happened to him during this quest?

It's not about you anymore, Conan, he reminded himself bravely, but still the urge to turn around and go home to a big bowl of Fancy Dinner was overwhelming. Torn, he turned around to face the direction he had come.

Conan went completely blank and considered the terrible possibility that the damage to his superior feline radar had not been temporary. Maybe his navigational skills were suffering long-term damage from the lunch-box jostling.

He had no idea where he was. Worse, he didn't know where Justin lived and he wasn't sure where home was either.

Fear shot through him, but Conan knew he had no choice now but to follow his shaky intuition and continue on to where he thought Justin's house might be.

I am going to find him or die trying, he decided courageously and then tacked on a tiny little prayer just in case the Great Cat Spirit was listening. *If I do die trying, my only request is that the end not come from starvation.*

Or a dog.

Or a car.

Or drowning.

Or a skunk. Oh, especially not a skunk. That would be second on his list of ways not to die. Right after starvation.

What life was he on anyway? He really had to stop and figure that out before he did anything else rash.

The truth was, he had to stop because the list of possibilities for the ways one small cat could meet his demise had shaken him badly. Conan sat down to have a little rest. He meowed weakly, but it seemed no one heard him.

Not even the Great Cat Spirit.

Chapter Ten

Justin could barely see over the flowers he had stuffed into the cab of his truck with him. He had stopped at the flower shop after work and cleaned them out. There were flowers to say he was sorry he had behaved badly and flowers to say he loved her. There were flowers that reminded him of the color of her lips and there were flowers that would match her hot-pink toenails.

Now that he had decided he was doing this love thing, he was going whole hog. He was going to do it right. Tomorrow he was taking her shopping for a ring.

He stopped in front of her house, aware of the most delicious sense of homecoming, aware of how eager he was to see her, aware that he had even missed the stupid cat.

The house looked closed up and dark. He knew she was home because he had called the library and been informed she was not at work again today. He knew she was home, even though she would not answer her phone.

Well, he knew how to soften her up. He hopped out of his truck and loaded up his arms with flowers. They spilled out of his arms and left a trail behind him up her walkway. He finally made it to her front door and dropped a few more blossoms as he freed a hand to push her doorbell.

And then pushed it again.

After a very long time, the door opened just a crack.

"Go away," she said.

For a moment he felt that familiar aggravated feeling with her. Couldn't she see that he was going down on one knee? Didn't she understand what this meant?

He caught a peek of her and his heart plummeted. She looked like death—her face pale and splotchy, her eyes swollen, a light gone from her.

His anger evaporated. Had he done that? Had he done that to her?

She closed the door.

"Bridget, I am not going away."

Silence.

He set down his flowers and went back to the truck for more. As he came up the walk, he saw a little flick of her front-window venetians. Then they closed.

A sane man might have understood he was being spurned, but Justin realized he had let sanity scatter to the wind a long time ago. He made one last trip to the truck, retrieved a house plan, then settled on her porch swing, opened it up and began to study it.

After a long time her door opened a crack. "Go away," she said. "I'm not coming out."

"I'm betting sooner or later you will. You have to get groceries sometime."

"They deliver," she said and closed the door.

The sun dipped in the sky. A chill came into the air. Darkness fell.

"Bridget?"

Silence, though he knew she was right by the window. "I'm going to have a pizza delivered. You want some?"

No answer. He went to his truck, placed the call on his cell phone.

If the pizza delivery boy thought it was strange for a man to be sitting on the front porch by himself, surrounded by flowers, he must have sensed his tip would be jeopardized to say so.

"I bet Conan would like some of this pizza," Justin called.

No answer.

He left a few pieces for her and her cat, went and got a jacket to ward off the cold, settled into her front porch swing for the long haul. At some time he must have dozed. The swing settling beside him woke him up. She was wrapped in a blanket, sitting as far from him as she could get.

He was careful not to make any fast moves.

"Conan is gone," she said, not looking at him. "He's been gone for two days. I looked for him all day today. I have ads on the radio and in the paper. He's not coming back, Justin."

Here he was making his stand for love, and she was going to talk about the cat? Then he recognized they were at a place they had been before. And he recognized love asked him to choose differently. When she had told him on Saturday morning that her cat was sick, he should have gone in the door, not down the steps. He should have recognized her fear was real and that love sometimes required a man to put his own agenda on hold, to put other people ahead of himself.

So now he was being given that same choice to make again, differently this time.

"Why didn't you call me?" he asked. "I would have helped you look for Conan."

A sniffle. "I didn't think I'd ever hear from you again."

"No such luck. Bridget Daisy, I'm so in love with you, I'm going to sit on this porch until the end of time unless you agree to love me back."

"Don't, Justin," she whispered.

"Don't what? Love you?"

"I can't love anything else," she said. "I gave it a try with the cat. And he's gone. Everything that I love goes away and it doesn't come back."

Like a man taming a wild horse, he sensed her fear and her skittishness. Slowly, slowly, slowly, he closed the gap on the swing between them, took the smallness of her hand in his. It was cold.

The sniffle became a sob. And then her head was tucked into his shoulder. And she was telling him about being a little girl, waiting for her daddy to come back home, looking out the window, waiting for the phone to ring, haunting the mailbox.

Then she was silent, her tears wetting through his shirt to his chest.

He felt her sorrow to the depths of his soul. He

wasn't quite sure what to do with it and so he did his best to listen to his heart.

Softly he said, "Bridget, I'm not going away. Not ever. I'm going to love you and look after you and protect you and make you laugh until the day I die."

She pulled back and looked at him, fear and hope mingled in the gorgeous depths of her green eyes. And then she sighed, the sound of a person who had held their breath for a long, long time.

"Thank you, Justin," she whispered. "Thank you for saying that."

"I'm going to marry you," he said, "even if you do come part and parcel with the world's most annoying cat."

"I don't think he's coming back, Justin. He's been gone since yesterday morning. He might have even left Monday night."

"If he can be found, I'm going to find him," Justin vowed. "And if I can't find him, I'm going to be here to help you deal with the loss. Do you hear me? I'm going to be here for you, Bridget."

She nodded and said softly, "I hear you, Justin."

And he knew she did. He knew her heart had heard him. But it was time to get on with more pragmatic matters. "Tell me what you've done so far to locate Conan."

By three in the morning he was regretting that he might have given her false hope about finding the cat. With a flashlight he had searched every ditch and piece of woods within two miles of her place. She'd been by his side for most of that, but he had finally insisted on taking her home.

He had tucked her into bed, kissed her gently on the cheek.

"It's okay if you don't find him," she said.

But somehow he had to find that cat. To prove to her that love and loss were not always tragically intermingled. But his search turned from hours to days, and by the fifth day the cat had been missing, he began to resign himself to the fact they might not find it.

Through those days of searching he and Bridget grew closer. She showed him she had a surprising tendency for toughness under that tender exterior, though maybe he should have known that from the day she threw the hammer at him! She showed him she was deep and kind and intelligent and beautiful in ways he had not understood before. His commitment to her deepened every day.

"Justin," she finally said, her effort to be courageous endearing her even further to him. "Give up. Conan's gone. He's not coming back."

But giving up was not part of Justin's nature.

As a desperate last measure, he called an old friend. Gus kept cougar hounds.

"Here's the thing," Gus said an hour later, in front of Bridget's house with three slathering smooth-haired dogs throwing themselves on the ends of leashes and yipping impatiently. "They'll follow the scent of a cat and they can pick up old trail. Nearly a week old? I don't know. Maybe. We haven't had any rain. But with each day there is more chance the scent trail will have been contaminated, crossed by another more recent scent that will be more attractive to them. I guarantee these hounds will turn up a kitty, but I can't guarantee it will be the right one."

"A poor chance is better than no chance," Justin said.

"As near as I can figure, Conan went through that cat door and over the fence right here. See the prints in the dirt?"

Gus brought the dogs to over to where Conan's paw prints were preserved deep in the dirt under the fence. The yipping changed in tone and volume. One of the dogs let out a long, eerie bay. All three began lunging against the leashes, nearly pulling Gus over.

Gus handed him one of the leashes. "Don't let him loose, whatever you do. This dog ain't been trained to be kind to cats."

Noses down, the dogs began to run in frantic circular motions. When they caught the scent, they would bay and lunge forward with such incredible enthusiasm that Justin thought his arms might be removed from their sockets.

Four hours later he was absolutely exhausted. The dogs were as enthused as they had been at the beginning, lunging, tongues lolling, baying more and more loudly, the bays closer together.

"That means the scent is getting fresher," Gus said.

Justin and Gus, pulled by the dogs, had been up alleys and through backyards. They had crossed main thoroughfares. Weirdly the serpentine pattern across town seemed to be bringing them closer and closer to Justin's own house.

At a park only half a block from his house, the baying took on a nearly hysterical note.

"Close to something," Gus said.

The dogs plunged into a wooded area of the park and stopped at a fallen tree. Howling and shivering with ecstasy, the lead dog began to dig.

"Pull him off there," Justin shouted. He handed over his own leash, and while Gus tried to control the frenzied dogs, he went down on his knees and looked under the fallen tree.

Two huge green eyes looked back at him.

"Conan?" he crooned softly. "Is that you?"

The eyes drew deeper under the log. Justin took a deep breath and put his arm in. Bracing himself to be scratched, and badly, he grabbed a handful of fur.

There was no resistance as he dragged the cat out from under the log, keeping his hand on its neck. They stared at each other for a minute.

The cat was orange, but all other similarities to Conan did not exist. It was bedraggled and if not exactly skinny, not fat either. Its fur was matted with mud and leaves and sticks.

"Is it the right cat?" Gus asked over the fiendish howling of his dogs.

"I don't think so," Justin said slowly, but he was aware that even if that cat looked wrong, something felt right.

And then he noticed the patchiness around the cat's ears, where the hair was growing in differently. Faintly Justin saw the patches were the outline of where a bandage had once been.

"Conan!"

He picked up the cat and rocked him against his chest. The cat was very, very still and then it breathed. And then it snuggled deep against his shirt and began to purr rapidly, like a child who had been crying, trying to catch his breath.

"You got the right one after all?" Gus asked, incredulous.

"This is him," Justin said and he felt the warmth of gratitude seeping through him. It was really nothing less than a miracle that he had found this cat.

The cat that had really begun this whole journey. For without Conan, there would have been no need for a cat door. And without a need for a cat door, there would have been no need for a contractor. And with no need for a contractor, there would have been no way Justin would have ever found her.

The one he loved. The one his heart had waited for all the days of his life.

Suddenly Justin wondered if it was any accident that the cat was so close to his house. Was it absurd to think Conan had been trying to find him, trying to bring him and Bridget back together?

Of course it was absurd to think that. He was tired and deliriously happy. The combination was making him think whimsically.

Still, looking at Conan, the cat's green eyes fastened on his face with such intensity, something in Justin insisted on acknowledging a truth that rational thought would probably never confirm.

"Thanks, buddy," he said softly. "Now let's go home."

He noticed the cat shivered every time the dogs renewed their barking and so he opened his shirt, tucked Conan right inside next to his heart, buttoned the shirt securely around him and folded his arms protectively around the quivering bundle of fur.

Conan had thought it was all over, nine lives gone. Shivering pathetically in the damp, dirty hole beneath a fallen log, exhausted, hungry and frightened, he had heard the baying of the dogs drawing nearer and nearer.

Suddenly a grotesque snout had poked into the hole's entrance, black and wet, quaking with excitement, the dog near-delirious in his anticipation of the kill.

This is it, Conan had thought, resigned. Death by dog, after all. He was so miserable that it seemed, frankly, like a better way to go than starvation. Though how cruelly unfair that his last whiff of earthly air had to be filled with the stench of beast breath.

He had closed his eyes and braced himself for the hound's hideous fangs. Was it going to hurt? Or would it be quick?

The stench had ceased abruptly.

That was painless, Conan thought. *Am I dead?*

Cautiously, he had half-opened one eye. Human hands, big and male, groped around inside the hole. He shrank back, wanting to attack, but finding he had neither the physical ability nor the mental willingness. He went limp as the hands closed around him and dragged him toward the light.

Temporarily blinded, Conan had trouble focusing on his rescuer/capturer/executioner. He'd had to blink several more times before he got it. The Pest! He did not think he would ever have been so happy to see Justin West. More surprising was how happy Justin West looked to see him!

Conan wondered how close he had actually come to finding Justin, instead of the other way around.

As if reading his mind, Justin said, grinning, "Hey, buddy, you're half a block from my house, almost as if you were trying to find me."

With that Conan began to purr. Recognition at last! This man understood him. Understood how smart and brave he was, what lengths he would go to to do the right thing. As they had gazed into each other's eyes, any last bit of resentment Conan had harbored melted. He knew that this was the one man he could share his home and Miss Daisy—with.

Tired as he was, Conan could not resist poking his head over the protective barrier of Justin's arms. He stuck out his tongue at the hounds who still strained at their leashes.

Then, totally spent, he snuggled deeper in Justin's arms, and unleashed a torrent of ecstatic purrs. It occurred to him that maybe this was one of those stories with a happy ending after all.

From her front window, where she was keeping vigil, Bridget saw Justin coming down the walk, way behind that strange man with the repulsive dogs.

There was no cat with them, and she felt her heart plummet.

And then she felt it grow strong again as she watched him come toward her house, watched the unconscious strength of his stride. One man in a million would have done what Justin just did for her. He had put his whole busy life on hold to undertake a nearly impossible mission—to find her cat.

And that one man in a million loved her. He had said he would be there for her no matter what. And he had proven it beyond a shadow of a doubt in the tension and worry of the last few days.

His calm and consideration had been unfailing. His declaration of love alone had been able to pierce the fog of worry and anxiety she was in. Justin West had asked her, Bridget Daisy, to marry him. It was like sun shining behind storm clouds, promising a better day.

As Justin drew closer, Bridget ran out the door, right past the man with the dogs. She flung herself against Justin and reached up on her tiptoes. His face was covered in grime and salt, and she kissed it over and over again.

"I love you," she said once softly and then louder. She realized she didn't care who heard her. She didn't care if it was on the front page of the newspaper tomorrow. She was going to marry Justin West.

It suddenly occurred to her that he was smiling strangely and that there was a funny warm lump in his shirt.

She reeled back from him, and a little tip of orange fur emerged in the V where his shirt met his throat. Two large ears popped out, and then slowly and suspiciously a cat peeked out.

Her heart stopped. She held her breath. Could it be?

Of course it was! Laughing, tears flying down her face, she undid the buttons of Justin's shirt.

"I always hoped this would happen in a different context," he teased lightly.

"It will," she promised him and hefted Conan out of his shirt. She gasped at the condition of her cat. He had lost pounds of weight and his coat was bedraggled, but she would know him anywhere.

"It will?" Justin growled in her ear.

"I'm going to marry you, Justin West. I'm going to marry you and drive you crazy all the rest of your days. I'm going to take you to poetry readings and Shakespeare plays. I'm going to learn to play pool and fish. Oh, Justin, I can't wait! Do you know how long it's been since I felt that way about life? As if I couldn't wait?"

Justin leaned his forehead against hers. "I can't wait either. For you to undo my shirt for real. For little green-eyed babies and—"

The cat meowed plaintively.

"Justin, where did you find him?" Bridget breathed.

"About half a block from my house. Bridget, this may sound crazy, but I think he was trying to find me. I think he was trying to bring me back to you."

Her heart did the most tender little flip-flop and she smiled softly at *her* man. Of course, it was crazy to believe that. What kind of man would assign such a complex motive to a simple cat?

A man who was a secret romantic, that's what kind of man. A man who was so, so strong, and who used that strength to shield the tenderness of his heart. The kind of man who would say something like that was, quite simply, the kind of man she could love forever.

The cat meowed again.

"He's starving," Bridget said. "Let's get him something to eat."

"There's pizza left."

The cat sighed and purred and sighed again. He snuggled deep into Bridget's arms, but his eyes were fixed on Justin West, and the light that glowed in them was unmistakably adoring.

Epilogue

Three months later, Bridget stood at the back of the church, trembling. The bride's side of the church was full. She hadn't thought she knew this many people, but it seemed the whole town was determined to see their librarian get married. All the regular patrons of the library were here, plus every member of the poetry club. Myrtle, thankfully, had not volunteered to recite. And on the other side of the church were all Justin's friends, looking uncomfortable with freshly cut hair and in freshly cleaned suits.

The two sides of the church were eying each other with mingled curiosity and wariness.

Fred patted her arm. "Don't be nervous," he said to her. "He's a good, good man."

"I know," Bridget whispered.

"And you are a good, good woman. You deserve each other. You belong together."

"I think we do."

"Ya see, you both been through hard things," Fred said gently. "It's written all over you. We don't have power over what comes in our lives. There will always be hard things that we can't control. The world brings good people bad things. It brings floods and fires and accidents. It brings your pappy leaving you as a babe, Justin's daddy getting sick and becoming a stranger to his own son."

Bridget's trembling stilled as Fred's warm, wise voice washed over her, soothed her. She was so pleased that this wise and wonderful man had said he would be honored to walk her down the aisle. In the last months she had come to know him so well and appreciate him so deeply.

"The only thing," Fred continued, "we have power over is the kind of people we choose to be. We don't get to choose the crisis, but we get to choose who we will be in the crisis. You remember that. When money is tight or the baby is crying or the basement is filling up with water. You remember to choose who you are going to be."

Babies, she thought, *babies with Justin.* Not right away, but someday. A warmth began to wash over her.

"I will, Fred," she said. "I'll remember that forever."

The wedding music began, and she chose to hold her head high and be a woman who was willing to stake her life on love, even though it was not the safest of choices. She chose to be a woman walking toward the future she saw shining in Justin's eyes. She had to remind herself to walk slowly, because she wanted to run. She wanted to run to him.

She remembered the handful of treats in her hand and she discreetly dropped them onto the floor to give Conan a path to follow.

She walked down the aisle, white silk and lace swirling around her.

Fred leaned close and whispered, "And you remember one more thing, Bridget. You remember, when your heart is troubled, when you can't see your way clear, you will always be sent what you need. Sometimes it's hard to recognize what it is that you've been sent, but if you look with an open heart, you will always see it."

What she saw was her groom, the man who had been sent to her closed-up little world to set her free. She looked into Justin's face, into the hazel eyes made brilliant by love, and the world faded for a moment, until a ripple of laughter filled the church.

She knew what had happened and she and Justin grinned at each other. It had been taking a chance to include him in the ceremony, but they wanted their wedding to reflect how they wanted their lives to be. And that meant taking chances and having fun. It meant being lighthearted but never ignoring the things that were important to them.

She turned to look and she saw the funny little miracle that she had been sent when she'd needed it most.

Conan was trundling down the aisle. His little black tuxedo was on crooked and looking a little worse for the wear after his last rather vigorous attempt to escape it. The ring basket, attached to the tuxedo with velcro, was slipping precariously to one side.

He looked absolutely mutinous. He even glanced over his shoulder and squinted at the back door. Bridget held her breath until Conan discovered the trail of treats. Then he made his way unerringly toward the front of the church.

Suddenly he seemed to realize he was the center of attention. He paused here and there to preen. He accepted a pat, rubbed a leg, glared balefully at Duncan Miller, who declared just a little too loudly he had never seen such an enormous cat.

And then he was beside them. And Fred rescued the rings, picked Conan up and tucked him under his arm.

The minister began. There was a huge smile on his face—because of the cat or because of the love that shone like hope for all mankind from that young couple in front of him, it was hard to tell.

"Dearly beloved…."

Even Conan grew very still, as if he understood the age-old sacredness of the ceremony.

"Who gives this woman?" the minister asked.

And Fred said firmly, "I do."

But his voice was very nearly drowned out by another.

It said, "Meeecce-ow."

* * * * *

COMING NEXT MONTH

#1802 DOMESTICATING LUC—Sandra Paul
PerPETually Yours

Puppy's got his work cut out for him when he meets his new owner, Luc Tagliano. Though grieving his lost mistress, Puppy wants this thickheaded human to see how good regular playdates with kind and patient animal trainer Julie Jones could be....

#1803 HONEYMOON HUNT—Judy Christenberry

When he hears that his wealthy father is globe-trotting with some new bride, Nick Rampling senses a gold digger's snare and teams up with Julia Chance, the bride's prim daughter. But their cat-and-mouse hunt for the couple soon convinces him it's *their* hearts that are in flight!

#1804 A DASH OF ROMANCE—Elizabeth Harbison

Run out of her catering gig by an evil queen of a boss, Rose Tilden relocates to a neighborhood Brooklyn diner. But when the handsome developer Warren Harker shows interest in the area, she learns that even the chaotic stirrings of love can create intoxicating flavors....

#1805 LONE STAR MARINE—Cathie Linz
Men of Honor

How could ex-marine captain Tom Kozlowski mistake her for a stripper-gram? Feisty schoolteacher Callie Murphy's anger cools when she sees the pain in his eyes. And as she reaches out to this wounded warrior, she's soon wondering if he can't teach *her* something powerful about the human heart....

SRCNM0106